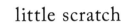

little scratch

little scratch

A novel

REBECCA WATSON

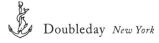 Doubleday *New York*

All rights reserved. Published in the United States by Doubleday,
a division of Penguin Random House LLC, New York, and distributed in Canada
by Penguin Random House Canada Limited, Toronto.

www.doubleday.com

DOUBLEDAY and the portrayal of an anchor with a dolphin are registered trademarks
of Penguin Random House LLC.

Jacket photograph Tamara Staples
Jacket design Emily Mahon

Library of Congress Cataloging-in-Publication Data
Names: Watson, Rebecca, [date]- author.
Title: Little scratch : a novel / by Rebecca Watson.
Description: First edition. | New York : Doubleday, [2020]
Identifiers: LCCN 2019054623 (print) | LCCN 2019054624 (ebook) |
    ISBN 9780385545761 (hardcover) | ISBN 9780385545778 (ebook)
Classification: LCC PS3623.A8733 L58 2020 (print) | LCC PS3623.A8733 (ebook) |
    DDC 813/.6—dc23
LC record available at https://lccn.loc.gov/2019054623
LC ebook record available at https://lccn.loc.gov/2019054624

MANUFACTURED IN THE UNITED STATES OF AMERICA

10 9 8 7 6 5 4 3 2 1

First American Edition

For James

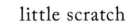

little scratch

I am travelling through, passing my own capillaries, red lines rushing by,
more red, caverns in my periphery like hulled strawberries, feeling a pain
across my body (which I am in, am travelling through), tingling then sharp,
sawlike, moving across me, rhythmic, back and forth, raking as I travel,
beginning to emit a melodic sound

                                        sounding

singing? is my body singing? is it in my veins?   (raking)   rising

the sound is growing louder   (raking)   rising

as I continue travelling, reddening,   (raking)   rising

speeding past another pathway, carrying more blood this way and that as
I fall through my own body until

                    light!

sound loud and wait   rising   rising   raking

wait

no   nails in skin

          no!   alarm sounding

no! fucking dream tricking me into fucking scratching my own skin! fuck!

my head!weight   heavy on my eyes   tight head

slipping in and out   alarm stop!   tapping phone

                                              dry mouth

slipping in and out wish it was as liquid as it sounds slipping in and out

    instead of this   lurching   this   crawling   back to   sleep

crawling back through red to   his face   looming   (inside my head)
can see my own face too, even though I'm in my own body, inside my head,
so I don't know why I'd be able to see my own face and yet, can see clearly,
it wincing, and my stiff limbs, body completely still, no, stiff, still sounds
too calm, it wasn't calm, can't have looked it, no,

and there's my mouth,   I know, I know how this plays out

no   no   not now   no   no

        away from this   not this part

focus on afterwards,   afterwards, though it can't have been straight after,
must be skipping here, something skipping, because the afterwards I
remember is outside, outside when I felt that strange freezing, burning,
hot sore yet freezing   the shock   of that

        christ

    christ

    celebrating another fucking morning by waking up like this

how many now? dozens?   crawling awake now

more than that   awake for real now, get up for real now

no more thinking about that now   dry mouth and warm in bed

how long   so warm

has my phone   so   warm

been   ugh   grabbing phone

snoozing!   oh god   **07:40**

must! get! up!   (skin burning)

blood under my nails from fucking scratching in my sleep

fucking hell, fuck's sake   the taste in my fucking mouth

head face down on pillow soft   waaaaaaaaaarm

got to do this thing again, the waking up thing, the day thing, the work thing, the disentangling from my duvet thing, this is something, this is a thing I have to do then,

rolling over, sitting up, my head moving forward faster than I thought I was moving it

sitting up

bra on floor, dress one step further back,

can trace my path to the bed last night (I didn't even drink that much!)

water   (my head disagrees)

pint glass by bed   glugging

ah, sweet water   glugging

toes out from under duvet now

                        (then back under)

following the pattern of my eyes (open, shut / back, forward)

legs out now, feet onto floor, moving now and   up

standing, walking   (swaying a little but catching self)

across corridor   bare soles on wood

heavy head   heavy head   into bathroom

door shut, lock, yanking shower handle

dragging pants down   t-shirt off

in   to   hot! hot!

pushing down handle   hot!   ah   better

eyes closed   water over head, body yes yes yes

yes this

hands over hair   smooth, wet, not my own

not my body, not my own

popping cap, lathering hair (that is not my own)

yes this

rubbing eyes soap falling, watching it run over my nipples,
into my tummy button

collecting by my feet   it's Friday!

(none of these are mine)

                          hands in hair

                          soap slowing

                          closing eyes

head   clearing   clear-headed (foggy but clear)

(running hands over not my hair)

pushing down handle   not thinking about that

cold   nope not that

cold!   so tired, tired of not sleeping, then sleep, then

awake! remembering, sleep, wake!

shower off, and body now mine, othering sheen lost (hints of it left in the
drops across my body)

(that is back to being mine)

wringing hair   always so much water!

cold   out   towel,

rubbing, covering

hearing a tapping,   peeking   grey   it's fucking raining

great   feeling loaded

wriggly

the familiar feeling of a hangover poo

which is fortunate really, as I'm running   still a little wet,

late, that I'm hungover that is, as it'll speed up   sitting on toilet seat

the poo time, although there is an argument   towel on lap,

to be made (I'm not   leaning forward

making it) that the hangover

freeing emptying

and the running late have rather   hearing,   plop!

a significant correlation, but as I   (then faster)

said, I'm not making that argument   hearing   plop! plop! plop!

a little quicker than expected

Wiping, wiping, up and towel round flushing (stodgy toilet ignoring) unlocking

padding back over wood

drip

drip   drip

drip

drip   drip

into room, time   **07:56**

fifteen minutes, cool, cool, I got this   text from my him, no time to read

wardrobe open,   pants first

bra, shoulder, shoulder, clip, on

dress, off hanger

over head

tights, where tights, fuck no tights   must   cover   legs

floor   there!   inside out   will do will do

up leg, up leg

snapping at waist

mirror   oh god   black smears

face wipe, rub rub rub

getting rid of mascara to clear a space to put more on (not thinking about
that endless circle right now please and thank you), by mirror, mascara

shoop!

(out of tube)   left eye

blinking onto wand, winking

really, wink wink wink, right

eye, more wand, wink, wink,

wink, shoop! popping into bag

what else do I need for my his tonight   time   **08:00**   eek

pants, shoving in, jeans, jumper, shoving

right, right   teeth! sort this mouth out   back into bathroom

(shit! left pile of pants and t-shirt in here!),   toothbrush loading, water,
into mouth

looking in mirror as brushing   brushing   brushing

dragging hands through hair (wet) brushing, brushing, brushing, brushing,

dragging, dragging, dragging,   brushing, brushing, brushing, brushing,

brushing, spitting, rinsing,

spitting, rinsing, rinsing

grabbing pile   back to room

into washing bag on door

shoes!   shoving feet in   push, wiggling in, push, wiggle in

jacket on,   purse keys phone cool

time   **08:09**

right

      right

           down

                stairs (bag on back)

                    into kitchen (gross, pans, ignore)

grabbing apricot from shelf
(third down, my shelf), back out

slowing now, I've done it, I'm getting out of the house

taking bite   getting out!

      wait   I'm getting out!

no

eurgh!

it tastes like egg!

why! does it taste like egg!   perhaps

        because   two minutes ago

                                                I brushed my teeth

(although egg is a strange side effect)

either way, there it is   (egg)

slamming front door (pulling it shut, I would prefer,
                    but it needs slamming really)

and yep it's raining   June! raining! June!

put the apricot in the outside bin and   pick

It was my intention, just now, anyway   up

to put it in the bin, which, I believe,   my

is the important thing, the key thing to focus   pace

on, my intention that is, but unfortunately   to the station

there are other factors to consider   for you see

the lid of the bin has a lot of water settled on top,

and I have keys, a bag and

                such things

that make hand   agility   more   difficult

                                especially with the apricot too, leaking

                                                        juices

propped in my hand between thumb and finger

(in that little pocket your palm can create)

and so, just now, you see, I could only open the bin lid

> just so wide   without
>
> dropping anything
>
> (apart from the apricot)
>
> (which I wanted to drop)
>
> (in the bin)

    and, you see,

I could only open the bin lid

> just so wide   without
>
> spending too long
>
> stationary in the rain

so, really, if you're fair, you can excuse me that even though my intention was to put it in the bin, to slip it through the gap I had willingly (voluntarily!) created by raising the lid,

I can be forgiven for allowing the apricot to drop, to miss the gap, and for me to be okay to leave it by the bin (so close, really, to where it ought to be, that it isn't too much fuss)

especially as the

                    intention

was still   there,

and as I said, I do need to get to the station for my train to work, and the

overground runs   every   fifteen   minutes!

it's not like waiting for a tube

and of course it is likely that

when I'm next home a house

mate may say, curiously (or

perhaps

with a bit of irritation),

                    SOMEONE CHUCKED A PEACH BY THE BIN!

I won't correct them that it was an apricot

because that might give it away

if I know exactly what type of fruit it is, and

consider myself the authority even! no, I'll

nod my head and say   A PEACH! HOW WEIRD!

I'll wrinkle my nose with them (unable to

get another apricot out of the fridge to eat,

which I had entered the kitchen to do, in   I am wandering

case it was a bit obvious that the criminal,   yes, so, peach,

the disgusting fruit thrower, was in front   no

of their very eyes)   apricot, walking and the rain is calming more like spitting although always a weird way of describing rain (spitting rain isn't much like spitting, that would be large sporadic globules, erratic enough to leave space for the sky to take a break and suck it all back in and up) but yes walking   walking   walking

walking	raining	walking	walking	raining	walking
meat and	chips, £3	checking	phone	**08:20**	got time
walking	walking	walking	walking	walking	walking
walking	walking	walking	walking	**08:22**	walking
walking	walking	walking	walking	**08:23**	walking
walking	walking	walking	walking	walking	walking
chicken	bones	on ground	walking	still partly	breaded
exposed	one side	to the	bone	walking	walking
walking	walking	like a	woman	showing	one
breast	walking	whilst the	other	walking	remains
tucked	away	walking	sort of	anyway	walking
walking	walking	walking	a man	is	
			slowing	slowing	slowing
walking	he's not	walking	he's	driving	driving
walking	raining	walking	in his	car	driving
walking	is he going	walking	driving	slowing	driving

walking   to say   walking   driving   slowing   driving

walking   something walking   slowing   slowing   slowing

walking   walking   walking   BEEP

walking   faster   walking   slowing   windows   rolling

            nearing   station   down

preparing   myself   to,   him,   *alriiiiiiiiiiiiiiiightt!*

my   middle   finger   raising

he can't drive his car onto the platform   it's okay   it's okay

raising   raising   raising   it's okay   it's okay

swinging right in, through entrance,   he's   gone

hearing him, muffled   *phark awff you bitch*

gladly sir

                                                08:27

soon, tight, but eaaaaaaasy   card out

tapping   beep

stairs

the

up

                            wiping wet cheeks

two at

a time

eaaaasy

onto platform, faces up, them seeing me, me seeing

my own face,

body, legs, etc

assessing the me which I cannot see but see them seeing

forgetting to assess them

because I am too busy assessing

what they're assessing,   walking

                                                 down

which I can't actually assess   platform

because there is no

full

length

mirror

balanced against nothing on the middle of the   walking

platform for me to use to assess my assessment   down

of their assessment to see if it is accurate, although,   platform

14

come to think of it, if I don't have time to assess

them, because I'm assessing me who they're assessing,

then who's to say that they're not doing the same –

assessing what I'm assessing, or, indeed, what they

assume I'm assessing, so we're all just assessing

what we assume they're assessing

i.e.

ourselves

which we cannot see,

although I still know that my face isn't quite worn into the day, tight, not
quite set, even if I c—THE TRAIN APPROACHING GURGLING
QUITE FAST AND EVERYONE IS STANDING STIFF AND

I AM GETTING TO   THE   LAST CARRIAGE

SWIFTLY STEATHILY WHERE THERE WILL BE A SEAT
(PLEASE BE A SEAT) ANd the   train   is   slowing

        [doors   opening]

                        seat!

bag off back

between legs

slight prickle on cheek

sitting !   opening my phone

sending text to my him,   (one already there from

                                            him: **GOOD MORNING!**)

                    me,   **GOOD MORNING!! absolutely**

consider sending emoji to evoke the   **scrambled onto the overground**

scramble, but not sure which one is   an egg? but he might not get that

quite right, so leave it   text from mum   was there last night and never
                                                opened

        shutting eyes, feeling lids puckering against my cheekbones

        then wide   clicking, open   **Long time since we caught up,**

        blinking   mouth clamped shut   **free tomorrow night for a**

everything pursed   wanting to hear her   **chat? Xxx**

but knowing she'll ask how's work   how are you waiting for information

can't face right now   thumbs over screen   moving next to each other

                    like they're conferring

but I'm not free! I'm out tonight!   easy **Sorry mum, going to this literary**

that's it, make it sound like my writing   **event tonight! Hoping to speak**

is bloody going anywhere   **to some helpful people. Let's talk**

                                    soon though xx

that'll do   for now   that'll do   flicking,

looking at my phone notes

(filled with the sort where a thought flies into your head that suddenly you know you must record, regardless of anything, in that moment, regardless of who's there or what is balanced in your hands, it is IMPERATIVE that you record this fragment)

(not the phone note sort where you say

OH YES, THAT BOOK SOUNDS MARVELLOUS!

and put the title in your phone

perhaps with the author's surname

and come across it three months later

try to recall its roots

ignore

a few more months later

glimpse

ignore

no not that sort)

One reads   **firwqks sex same thing a provess and end**

            huh

at the time, it was   a (!) revelation (!)

(when even was it?)

I was another me   !!

then   !a fireworks display is the PERFECT ANALOGY
                    FOR SEX!

                    !!

the surges, fiery, coming in waves, the finale after the push and pull and to
and fro, and the mixing up, displays always returning to the

              familiar, age-old goodies

(a Catherine wheel/you cupping my breasts as you fuck me from behind)

and I'm sure, as I'm thinking this, that this is astute! profound (?)

no one has ever thought this before   surely

even when they're planted firmly in front of a   fireworks display

no one has hit upon the comparison   fireworks! sex!

boy, I've got it and I'm reaching for my phone

sliding open notes, tapping keys whilst the

others have lesser thoughts, beer drinking,

whilst I'm analogy thinking

(a chiming rhyme I agree, even at the time it first appeared in my head, but
I allow it, it makes me feel like I'm finishing a soliloquy)

I must remember this,   I think

                    thought

but now, weary on the train, it is   not what I thought   at all

can't quite delete the note though maybe it's smarter than I realise?

                                                              marking it

                                                       back of my mind

                                      (maybe tweet it ?)

locking phone

used to use any train journey I had to write, tapping into my notes

       but   can't   right   now

what was it?   April? May?   one month? more?

since I've written?

not that long   really   but if I don't write again

that would be long   if this is the beginning of me never writing again

then the one month six weeks? is significant   as the start of nothing

as the start of some non-writing eternity

shrugging off   hangover   pressing down, turning me melodramatic

existential

just because of a few drinks

I know not just because of that   there is a woman opposite me,
                                                reading a book, resting

but let's say it is   the back right against the window,

                                              her head behind it, also

                                        right against the window,

her hand is sprawled across the front   so I can't read the title
                    and it annoys me

not being able to read the title   so I stare at her book   urging her
                        move your hand

my eyes say

                        move your hand

                        let me in

my hair was resting

but now it's perching

signalling to her

without doing much

that she must   move your hand

she's noticing, I notice, and must decide whether she likes the look of me
enough to inch her fingers across, ever so, just gently, enough that I can
peep, collect together the letters,

her fingers are moving! palm flattening!

                o   b   s

                c   u   r

                i   n   g

even more

so, in defiance

        I

u

   n

z

   i

p

      my bag

and bring out my own book. Hands over cover (no peeking, woman in
front of me, with your secretive book, and your head against the window)

opening to page

moving postcard	(yellow, perhaps a face although never
out of the way	quite sure, Miró, I think, although now
holding it tight to	I try to think I am not entirely sure
the front cover	of that either)

and begin!

reading,	**I walked down the hill, feeling the**
scratching the soft crease	**weight of my rucksack. I felt the eggs**
of my inner arm	**boiled this morning and wrapped in**

resisting the soft crease   *WE ARE NOW*

of my inner arm   *APPROACHING*

reading,   *SEVEN SISTERS*   wrapped in

kitchen roll, grow warm under a

sudden heat. It spread up through

the eggs, up through my water

pencil out of top pocket   bottle (now tepid, now useless,

interesting brackets   for I despise tepid water), and

drawing a line   (now tepid, now useless,

in the margin   for I despise tepid water), and

reading,   curled the pages of my book. The

thinking of my him, hoping   words smudged in the heat that is
he'll be wearing

his green jumper, feeling   now ricocheting from side to side,
a bit giddy now

thinking of my him and   melting the plastic of my pen. I can
if we'll get back late

feel it on my back too. Wetting my t-

wet?   shirt, leaking through into my spine.

Does the man   opposite me

know?

that I'm thinking about my boyfriend's   cock

                                       his face says nothing

inside of me?   (testing if his face reacts)   nothing

It would be surprising   but why would it?

admittedly   not everyone has to react

if he did   not everyone has to notice

        yet   now   I'm glad they don't

I fear he might

attempting to cut off my mind, just in case

like putting my

next   h

to   a

my   n

phone   d

shielding my texts,

I casually

    tilt

my head

away

ensuring that he cannot see me directly

so he does not know that I'm

(slightly wet)

imagining him   not you, man, with your jacket

(my him)   slightly wet from the rain,

hard against me   watching me

                                           (he wet, me wet!)

                     train stopping

filling   filling   filling   filling   filling   filling

    filling   filling   filling   filling   filling   filling

filling   filling   filling   filling   filling   filling

filling   filling   filling   filling   filling   filling

    filling   filling   filling   filling   filling   filling

filling   filling   filling   filling   filling   filling

filling   filling   filling   filling   filling   filling

    filling   filling   filling   filling   filling   filling

filling   filling   filling   filling   filling   filling

a kid! filling   filling   filling   filling   *mummy look at*
                                                            that dog!

who I cannot see!

but who

announces his presence

by announcing the presence

of

a dog

which I also cannot see

but looking round

everyone looking   I see

grumpy   grumpy   grumpy   grumpy   grumpy   dog!

except it is not a dog

not really

There is a man, hugging tight to him, a large teddy-bear

                                        dog!

Though I say teddy bear, it is not actually a bear,

a stuffed dog, I guess,

but that might sound like taxidermy (which it is not)

teddy bear still not right though

less floppy

more like

well

a dog

but larger, and, as I said, not a dog

I mean, it's meant to be a dog

but it is not a DOG

not a real one

The dog (not real) has its legs

tucked in on either side of

                    the man

            under   armpits

            under   arse

and the man is saying   nothing!

even though he must've heard the kid say   dog!

but   nothing!

he's closing his eyes now

resigned to the journey, body moving against

              the jerks of the train

I cannot fathom what a man,   his eyes still closed

unmoved by a child, would   hands gripped into fur

be doing on the way to Liv   is it Liverpool Street

erpool Street with a teddy   next? (I've lost count)

(not a bear)

dog (but not a dog)   *WE ARE NOW APPROACHING*

why are they   *LONDON LIVERPOOL STREET*   rustling

rushing already?   *WHERE THIS TRAIN WILL*   rustling

it's happening   *TERMINATE*   murmur

even now   of people getting ready

a distant murmur   preparing to feel rushed

even though the train is still

        moving   rushing

                    rushing

and it is, as it has been announced, approaching the

LAST STOP   rustling

it won't leave, turn back around, cement us back at   rushrushrush

Bruce Grove, because we hadn't zipped up   rushing

our bags before the door opened

I consider saying this,   (whilst not really considering

OI OI LADS!   because I'm not actually mad

SLOW THE FUCK DOWN!   or, at least, if I am, I'm not

IT'S NOT A RACE!   the confrontational sort

IT'S A FRIDAY MORNING! of mad, where I interrupt

TIME WILL PASS THE   others, ask questions, raise

SAME WAY, THE SAME   eyebrows, I'd be the quiet sort,

SPEED, SO CHILL YOUR more twitching than asserting   )

SHIT!   man

with dog

not

moving

still

still

me

him

still

whilst

the others

rush   rush   rush   rush   rush   rush   rush   rush   rush   rush

rush   rush   rush   rush   rush   rush   rush   rush   rush   rush

[doors   rush   rush   rush   rush   opening]

   rush   rush   rush   rush   rush   rush

      me   rush   and   rush   dog

        and   rush   rush   man

          rush   rush   rush   rush

             rush   rush

               rush

we

disembark   (bark! disem! bark!)

him just ahead, legs

of dog visible, tucked

in still

going through   suitcase gate   beep

me following,   beep

following   passively   I might add

                                                     (have added, now)

this is just my way to work, after all

although admittedly, cutting same path

through throng of faceless   IF YOU SEA SOMETHING THAT

up the escalator   (usually I'd   DOESN'T LOOK RIGHT SPEAK TO

legs above legs   get the stairs   STAFF OR TEXT THE BRITISH

past doughnut stand yes, okay, fine   TRANSPORT POLICE ON SIX

at top of escalator   but it's   ONE OH ONE SIX WHEEL

pinks, shiny, shiny,   still the   SORT IT

shiny, cream (that   right way   SEA IT SUET

I imagine is inside   to work)   SAUTÉD

them)

up, outside, man ahead   PRET

rain halted, only remembering

because ground wet, a little   SECOND PRET

glistening, shiny, shiny,

doughnut ground

              bearing   to the right

        man ahead (bearing to the right first)

with his not-a-bear-it's-a-dog-but-not-a-dog

I see   a homeless ?   ?   !

        a few bin bags   by a closed shop doorway

                                            feeling sad, quite

                                            affected by my own mistake

(not) following (not) following   thinking for a second, that a few

(not) following, we crossing road   bin bags was a slumped man

separately, me, him, dog round   with no home

waist, faded pockets on the back

him past Timpson's   me past Timpson's

face ahead (obviously)

his face I mean, not mine,

although mine is also ahead

but his looks steady

set,   stern?   tense, I'm not imagining it, tense   decent, though

fixed ahead   firm ahead   it's nice to follow
                                                      knowing his face

                                                      is decent

pedestrian man in shadow then   lit up   green!

not worrying   him crossing   me crossing

not shuddering   others crossing (towards us)

not holding my phone   (looking at dog) (not a dog!)

unlocked   me hoping dogman   two girls, one laughing ready to call   does not mind the

                          laughing, which is

                          not directed at him,   I don't think,

                          although I guess it is,

                          but it's not ha! that man!

                          instead, ha! a fake dog! so real

                          wrapped around a man

                               nothing more

well that's what I guess, although I'm not an expert on laughter, never
claimed to be either, but I'm pretty sure it's nothing more

                          he's walking with purpose, boy oh boy,

                          I'm a fast walker (so I thought) but he's

                          pacingalong,clippingpavement

                          notturningtonoticecoffee,windows,or

                          poshshopwithplantpotsorthejewellers

                          thatwearepastbeforeIevennotice

wearepast   oh! a jeweller's!   I think retrospectively

it's funny, I think, as I follow him   red front of

without following him, as this is my   another PRET

way to work after all, that

the difference

between walking and following   (for the moment)

is   just   intention   ?

he would be fair enough   (I guess)

to think   (to fear even?)   the gentle   tap

                                                     of

                                                     my

                                                     feet

                                                     behind

                                                     him

but then   no!   BANK STATION

and   he's   going   down

feet

        disappearing

                        first

(me slowing)   then knees

                        bum fading

                                paws,   back,

                                paws, head

and he's gone

just when I was beginning to imagine the

!

!   ACCUSATION   !

!

turning around (dog still wrapped

around), him shouting

STOP FOLLOWING ME! me,

small voiced,   but, but, but   him,

STOP, STOP, STOP   me,

but, but, but   (image dissipating as I hear a man   *put four eggs*

saying something about eggs which I've already   *into boiling water*

forgotten, but see him now, mouth shutting,

outside another entrance to BANK)   (how many entrances are there!?)

he's smoking beside his friend   I assume, friend

right leg against the railing   city opening now

initially seeming   streets wider

as if his thigh   me looking up

is double the size, pressed tight against his leg   up   widescreen sky pushing, flesh out,   struck by

                                                       how beautiful it is

converting sidewards   struck by

                                                       how irritating it is

that it is here,

here, with all these men in suits, all these watch shops, that I am

seeing beauty

    checking phone   text   mum, **Okay then, another time.**

                                       Hope everything is good xx

oh mum   just sending her kisses,   **xxx**

nothing more right now   nothing from my him

                                               two ticks, grey, unread

                         waiting for the status under his name to flash

                         show when he was active

                                  !

        not since 07:50 okay   guess he's still on his bike

                                       locking phone

glancing at watch,   wonder where   bearing right

missing time,   dogman   avoiding

glancing, missing   is heading   cycle path

35

approaching work

and (dreading)

(suppressing dreading)

I will make myself

a coffee (I decide)

let that routine

calm me

warm me

wake me

although I feel

awake and alert

and don't actually

agree that coff

ee gets me alert

maybe it's his

job, some sort

of film runner

delivering a

dog for a

scene with

a spoilt child

or maybe it's

for his son

or maybe it's

just his and he

likes to take it

out to let it see (it can't see)

London

a woman

eating a

croissant

walking

pastry in

her hair

replaced by

a teenager

(boy) with a

suitcase

and a peeling

belt round his

blue jeans

although it does

sometimes   j   i   t   t   e   r   me

shake me up, turn me upside down, and make it hard to keep my eyes settled,
as if they no longer belong to me,   WHOSE EYES

approaching   ARE THESE!

36

I know this last

path, subconscious

shifting off, nudging me

to get my access card

out, arriving! arriving!

HELLO! CAN

SOMEONE

CLAIM THESE

EYES THAT ARE

NOT MY OWN

THANK YOU!

SWIFTLY PLEASE!   closer

closer

entering, swish down

getting

round and round the sort of

too

ferris wheel (if it were on its

close

back), yes, fine, revolving door,

line of plants on either

side,   security guard, me,   *morning!*   *morning!*

simultaneous

a little awkward, the call

and response conjoined

so now we don't know who is the caller and who is the

responder

and in the place where the second   morning!   would usually fall

silence!

swiping card   beep

getting through, someone else behind,   *morning!*

                              security guard,   *morning!*

        well done them for getting it right

down the stairs on the right

                        past a poster of New York

                                now London

past lifts,

down into the   dreaded   corridor,

through   dreaded   swing doors,   why

past   dreaded   toilet,   am

kitchen on   dreaded   left,   I

dreaded desk   dreaded   desk   here

approaching (dread)

            desk

belting myself in for the day

                                        (metaphorically)

                                        I wonder though

                              what sort of job would involve

belting myself in   literally

I mean, yes, there are the obvious ones, taxi drivers, pilots, yes yes,

I meant more – same context, desk

    cafetière sitting by computer screen,

                but belted in,

            some sort of experiment

           I gue— *morning!*

colleague here, me,   *hi!*

thankful, sometimes   *I'm making mint tea*

that she breaks my thoughts   *want one?*

me,   *yes please!*

actually, no, I was going to make coffee

I don't want that now it's   her,   *in or out?*

an afternoon thing   what me,   *what?*

                      her,   *in or out?*

what the fuck does she   me,   –

mean?   ?   ?   her,   *the teabag! keep it in?*

oh!   me,   *oh!*

that is not a normal expression me,   *in, thanks!*

christ

password typed without even thinking to type it in

        (how many times have I done this before)

(I consider counting

        but also can't be bothered)

log   g   ing   on   and

loading   loading   loading

    loading   fuck's sake   loading   and

any   time   now   it   will

           WELCOME!

google chrome, double click

outlook, double click

emails

loading   loading   loading   any time now

sifting through	**table at Padella – book?**
eyes moving down	**URGENT: LUNCH TOMORROW**
deleting	**LEGAL COVER FROM 7PM**
sighing	**a few more lunch invites please?**
keeping unread	**need more printer paper**
to-do list only going up up up	**invites to be sent**

you can do that yourself

(I think whilst doing it)

deleting spam in between

not quite reading

just knowing

can you block out space in diary? –
I'm away next week
dictionary king Word of the Day Quiz
LoveDoctor89 horny chicks in your area
LinkedIn People looking at your profile

      colleague setting tea down   *here you go!*

uncheerily, me,   *cheers*

          nothing urgent   really

      opening phone   still nothing from my him

                saying,   **hey sweetheart**

knowing he's got a busy day   **I know you've got a busy day**

but wanting him to know I'm here   **and I hope your pitch goes well.**

might tell him I finished the book   **Looking forward to seeing you later**

he lent me? or maybe later   **xxxx**

he's busy   two ticks, delivered

getting banana from drawer   closing phone

quite browned   turning it over on the desk

splitting top off, snapping sideways

breaking its neck   pulling down its clothes

slither by slither

browned inside too   picking up tea

                sip   actually quite nice

     bite   actually quite nice

     bite

         sip

         sip

     bite

         sip

         sip

     bite

         sip   turning phone over

     bite   him there! so quick!

         sip

thanks babe

can't wait to see you later too! ♥

hope you got to work okay after

your scramble

!!   he has sent the egg emoji

   !   !

                    bite   me smiling

                                            turning phone over again

will reply in a minute   just a minute   give him a second

                looking around   no one looking

as I am struck   by my phallic breakfast chewing   and   gone

last swallow and   suddenly   feels   dirty

                        sticking on my throat

done this before at the desk

munching   munching   munching

like a child   eating a banana   (not thinking

                                just munching)

and then boss by desk   with that smirk

and him saying, that taste nice?

                that feel good?

me taking another bite then   later regretting

was it a statement?

                by taking a bite?

        obviously not   but still

question lingers even if I know the answer

                pulling slithers together now   resting on desk

                                        yellow and browns

        empty   next to the pack of Mentos (fruit)

        bought yesterday, one left, just the one, single one, to be eaten today

maybe I should lay it on the floor   the banana skin, that is

                            lay it just outside my boss's office

induce some cartoonish speculation   convince him he's actually inside
                                            a game of Super Mario Kart

play the theme tune in his office   lay out more banana skins

write GAME OVER on the glass of his door

watch you don't slip,   I'd say

you be careful now sir, don't make a slip-up now

us on either side of the banana skin   waiting to see   what
happens
                slip

                            me shaking head at own thoughts

                how did I get here   yes   skin

(not scratching my arm as I think about the banana skin on my desk)

        (which I am now moving off,

                                            standing up

                stepping to the side   few steps

                                            bin!)

44

bit of banana on my hand   wiping on chair   as I step (few steps) back

and   sit!

      sipping tea

      turning phone over

      typing,   ♥   ♥

wondering at what point I stopped thinking sending hearts was clichéd

and started doing it

started warming at the sight   of a

                      ♥

                 on my screen

closing phone   setting down   apple on it looking up

up off chair   (little springing sound)

back down corridor

into toilet

one cubicle closed   silence

me going to next one

        not scratching skin

tights down just a little

not uncovering knees

pushing self forward

peeing   muffling   peeing   peeing   against the side of the
                                               bowl

person in cubicle   still making no sound

telling me, clearly   in their silence   that they're waiting

                                             quietly clenching

                                           tense   in case they let

                                           anything

                                                    fall

                                           (I flush)

exiting cubicle pulling lock   hard (stuck?) then quick slamming across

                               sudden!   grating in my head

remembering   grooves   no

eyes shut   clearing head   open

pushing eyes shut   tight creased   open

to the mirror,   push, soap   waving hand underneath   nothing

                           waving,   nothing,   nothing

                                 water   !   spurting

                         hot, suds coming off back of

                                        hand, cascading from skin

studying face in mirror,   ignoring the silence of the clencher behind
                                   me, wiping   eyelash off cheek
                          biting lips   again ·   and again again

making them redden, willing them to spark, to plump, to do anything
other than   rest

as they are,   now   the same colour as my face,   bluer the longer I stare

shifting of feet behind me   imperceptible

the clencher flexing their toes, scraping soles against the grouting, me,
enough!

                    eyes off lips   (pinker now, awake)

snapping head, moving off, out of bathroom, back down corridor, down
down down to dreaded desk

leaning hand, elegantly poised over tea, fingers extending across the rim
– spider-like –

spindly, taking a few sips   (now cold)

noting teabag drifting, well, sinking,   buoy-like if a buoy were to sink, a
sack rather I guess, a jumper, waterlogged, almost tickling my nose

                                                takes a while to
with its edge, a watery hello,   get the image
thanking me for fulfilling its purpose,   now reaching   right

for The Spiker, a tool unlike many others   reaching

long-handled, silver, essentially a large (elegant!) hole-puncher

(so I guess it's like that, a hole-puncher I mean, and thus not a tool unlike many others, although I guess it could still be unlike many others, even if it is like a regular hole-puncher, but anyway, even though I did make the comparison, I wouldn't CAPITALISE hole-puncher, it is very much not capitalised, no emphasis, no aggrandising, but The Spiker? no question)

picking up the stacks of papers from the post trolley, putting The Spiker on top, carrying pile with both arms underneath

> as if I am a forklift,
>
> erect arms, carrying
>
> to

THE SPIKING STATION

> (referring to it majestically!   letting
>
> loud in my head! does not, sadly, make   pile fall
>
> it any less dull, but I have to try none   with a
>
> theless)   (quiet)
>
>   thud
>
>   onto side table

pulling twine from around the stack   red lines forced onto my palms, surprised by now that they haven't become permanent, that each day these lines fade without having time to notice how they disappear

> how many things   fade
>
>   hide!

                              under the skin

sorting   invisible to anyone else

              UK edition | New York edition

ready to add today's papers to the two piles of   pulling papers

papers that no one actually glances at, a well-   out,

hole-punched (spiked, actually, not hole-   flattening

punched) pile of newspapers for the journalists'   folds,

reference, if they so wish to use the spiking   approaching

station, as a reference for old articles, which   first

they do not, because of the   internet   pile

                                                      on

                              THE SPIKING STATION

untying string, laced through the pile, picking up The Spiker,

                         punching   ONE HOLE

                         punching   ONE HOLE

                         through newspaper,

threading string through   threading   ONE HOLE

                         threading   ONE HOLE

tying bow, one bunny ear, two bunny ear, crossing over and tied moving to a rhythm now, NEW YORK

untying string and then   punch   ONE

                                           punch   TWO

                                           thread   ONE

                                           thread   TWO

                    tying now, crossing over,   done!

twine on floor, grabbing loose supplements, scrunching   into bin

            picking up The Spiker   walking back to desk all spiked out

News Editor shouting something from far off (not to me but I still flinch),
them laughing, laughing, me all spiked out and them from a distance,
laughing (loud joke, not clear what, but something evidently is very funny
ha ha they say ha ha)

it's   checking phone   **10:38**

                        and I'm already all spiked out and them

                                ha ha ha ha, laughing

resting The Spiker back on the corner of my desk, noticing now it's a bit
like a librarian's desk   far off, distant, alone, keeping

                                                        check,

                                                        from afar

yes   afar   stressing it again

just in case I haven't thought enough about how isolated I am

going to cupboard behind desk now   notepads piled up, biros, uni-balls
                                                              (fine-points, code UB-157 in
                                                              BLACK and BLUE)

Nothing is wanting, it seems, the cupboard all full up, its belly sated, for
now, its rumbling paused (and I am delaying the day by thinking in cheap
metaphors, but here I am, with a cupboard patting its belly, filled to the
brim with A5 lined notepads)

sitting back down   chair springing

head now on those pads, those empty notebooks   is this what I do now?
Spike, check cupboard, stare at screen, with no sense of up, of escape
(of hope)   is this the new thing?   what will come sooner?
Telling someone? Telling my him?   or writing? my book that is, which
is not a book because it is not yet written and yet is that more probable?
        ?   ?

        it seems no answer is provided for that question

it seems I have to work out the answer myself but it is difficult when I
do not have access to certain information I need, for example, certain
information like:

        can I even write anymore?

        and, for example,

                is it a good idea to tell my him what happened and thus
                unleash questions and things and let it become someone
                else's thing too, what if he doesn't want to touch me, what
                if his eyes become pity, pity, pity and only pity

                what if what if pity fucking pity and then if I can't write,

and he can't stop seeing P I T Y whenever I open my
mouth or let my face settle for a second then what do I
have then? work? this place?

this dreaded fucking desk?   anything but that

look at me now lost in linearity, where is the freedom in my head, to not
have to only move side to side, stuck in straight lines every morning once
I've arrived in this office, breaking myself in every morning, having to
loosen the numbness   punch by punch

          but yes I can feel my head loosening, freeing, it's always this way,
numbness ebbs, visits, interrupts, but always pushed down   eventually
taking my head away, but always giving it back (or do I wrench it back?
I am not sure but I am tired certainly, so I might have been wrenching),
takes a while to unstick, colleague passing, who always makes tea for the
assistant in the corner, who, I wonder, perhaps knows everything, it seems
so, in her soft look, her incessant tea and the no questions, no questions,
apart from tea, and sometimes

noting things that she likes, today my shoes   her,   *nice shoes!*

patent t-bars that I rather like myself   me,   *aw, thank you!*

(obviously)   *they're from Tesco*
                                                                    but don't tell anyone

                                                          her,   *your secret's safe*
                                                                    with me

and she's away, me still not even sure what she does, her name beginning
with R, likely Rachel although that doesn't sound right,

someone called her over once after she left my desk (she was probably

pausing to offer me tea or compliment my dress), and I remember thinking
I MUST REMEMBER HER NAME but all that's left now is the R

I would conclude that she's imagined, except I imagine that if I were to
imagine people they'd make less small talk, do something more radical,
incite Gregorian chant, my subconscious trying to find an escape route, a
way to be sent out of this place for good (and a chant filling the newsroom
might do the trick), I don't think I'd imagine someone nice, I'd know I was
imagining it straight away,

nah I don't buy it,

I'd tell my imagined colleague,

just not a believable character I'm afraid, the critics would slate you
                    ignoring, admittedly, the fact that she does exist, her and
the flecked auburn falling across her back, the white of her eyes even
whiter than her skin

(her paleness not a weakness, not prone to illness, just   pale),

I'm still in my argument (with myself inside my head) ignoring the fact
that all of that exists, all of her exists, those eyes that hair those soft looks
that seem to say I know I know I know, all exist and thus she is believable,
is real even, but yes, after all, often those that are real are the ones that,
when imagined up, don't quite fit, don't quite work

and she is gone now after all

shoes still on my feet

her gone

wondering the difference between a woman saying   nice shoes a woman I do not know very well at all no and a man

I do not know very well at all   saying   nice shoes

                                    I guess

if a man says   a certain sort of man that is, I can't say for sure,
can't tell you how to know, just that you'll know when you know, that it's
that sort of man, yes,

when that sort of man says nice shoes

he is not   saying   nice shoes

he is   saying   I am itemising you

he is saying, take yourself out of that head and put your eyes in my sockets

because hello   I am itemising you

like   yesterday

that man rapping the side of his stand

selling caramel nuts   me sitting nearby   propped on the side by the
river   ten minutes before I needed to go back to my desk   reading
and then him, suddenly, rapping the side, rap rap rap, me head down
ignoring, him rapping the side, me looking up and   beaming at me,
nothing more, just wanting to grin, to show his presence when I was finally
for a moment not present anywhere

what are those moments called? some would call them niceties I guess but
I just hear the knock against the side of his stand with his fist (clenched),
needing me to notice, to be interrupted, to give the attention I was so set
on giving elsewhere

I know   if I told this anecdote   I'd stress the nuance,
if I were to tell my him about it, as I often end up doing, telling that is
(although not other things but this digression is not something I am going
into), I'd embellish, I'd say !HE LOOKED ME UP AND DOWN!, or
!he said PHWOAR LIKE A BIT OF THAT!, adding any detail to
support my side so there is no chance he'd doubt, no chance he'd say, Well
what's wrong with a man wanting to smile at you on a sunny day?
the answer is   obviously a lot   A LOT IS WRONG WITH
THAT   but I don't have the words   I can't unpick

right now   no words   just lines

remembering my him   ignoring the itch,

his birthday next week   ignoring its insistence

searching for somewhere to take him,   (opening new tab)

somewhere nice, near him, googling   **little dishes**

(it's the name of the place, although it sounds like a general enquiry)

Google confused suggesting random tapas,   **11:05**

          me clarifying   **little dishes, clapton**

TripAdvisor coming up,   **18, terrible**   clicking

instantly landing on a golden   **We were very excited to visit Little Dishes**

review, I can tell straight away   **which was we had heard about from Time**

from its density   **Out and was sure to be a lovely evening.**

          My Husband and I arrived at 19:25 for our

19:30 booking and were told to wait for our table. We then watched the staff member clear a table near us of glasses and then gestured to us to sit down. He did at no point wipe the table with a cloth, and there were several patches of crumbs in front of my Husband which he had to wipe off with his own hand. We knew they were busy so decided to give them the

[sic]

benefit of their doubt and choose just to continue our evening, hoping that things would get better. Unfortunately they did not. We were offered menus, after having to ask a passing staff member for

I'm tired, reading this

them, and were soon ready to order. I had looked at the menu beforehand and was excited to try the Braised Pigeon but when

dear god I'm tired

we ordered were told they had run out.

tired that there are people

There was no mark on the Menu and we

who actually write these things had not been told so I then had to go

56

people with money and no   through everything else, because they had
patience

who eat their pigeon   not stocked up enough pigeon though
(or equivalent

due to a shocking lack of   it was a friday night. Food arrived but I
pigeon) whilst

pondering how they will   had to send it right back because the steak
word their

dissatisfaction which they   looked raw and I had to ask them to cook
had already

decided to feel   it fully. My Husband's cauliflower was col-

there is   [more]

there is the option to select   [more]

but I ignore, thankful for the opportunity to stop, scrolling down further, a
few reviews for some reason in French, pithy captions here and there

BAD STAFF

and   ### CLOSED WHEN WE VISITED

I don't really want to see **hungarygeranium66**   unnerved, a little,

although I guess there's no chance she's going   that I cannot see

back so that might be the one place I can guarantee   my him right now

she won't be   I mean,

                obviously I can't, I'm here – at dreaded desk

and he is at his (un)dreaded desk   preparing his pitch right now?
                                     making coffee?

no, what I mean is, I guess, I can't   talking to a female colleague?

see his face. I could describe it   (no,

certainly, every detail   am certainly not imagining

(his body   that because it's not helpful

too)   is it no no no)

but I can't see it clear – don't have him here, don't have the things that
collect together, those specificities to make my him my him

as soon as we are apart, something flits – is absent – perhaps only exists ?

when we are together?   this thought is escalating

when we are perceiving each   and the sadness follows

other, renewing, creating what we see   building   as

                    I think

wait   if he dies then no more renewing   (building still)

just fading   pain initially   but then just   absence

can't rebuild, can't grow clearer, get that vision – all pieced together when
he says hello just fading fading   fading   jesus bleak fading

can you feel pain if you can't remember them with clarity? will my
mourning just turn to numb embarrassment? mourning that I can't

mourn? mourning the fading?

mourning where that swell used to be   just inside   then to no feeling
absence?   I don't like to imagine this, my him dead   of course I
don't

but I am, it seems,

I guess I might die first, be saved from it, but what about my him?
I think   I'd rather

                                            numb, mourn, fade, empty

than let   (my) him   numb, mourn, fade, empty

is that love?   probably   although I'm numb now anyway

not for my him, just me, inside, all over   a constant process of
                                        numbing and falling and

                                        stilling

my him occasionally pulling me back (big inhalation, and I'm here!)

                                        (grinning momentarily)

before I sink again   again   again   feeling – up through my legs –
a tingling

no   tingling   must   ignoring

                              ignore

                              legs

wondering how others are feeling after last night   ignoring legs

which was not, as I've acknowledged, a heavy one, and yet   ignoring legs has that haze

happy though   safe territory   there were no how are yous

or   what's new!

or   you MUST tell me EVERYTHING!

just beer and jokes more jokes, stories drowning out the following
(overlapping) (some repeating), me sarcastic, dry, delivering the right line
to pass things on

they didn't even notice that they learnt nothing new about me (which at
one time might've annoyed me, but last night dear god thank christ etc –
gratitude! a victory! a freedom!)

didn't scratch the whole way home   ignoring legs

even though I was in a train carriage   that, nowadays

all on my own   is my sort of

rolling eyes at the performance in my head   success
as I

clock   poster on the wall, just

                                              beyond

                                              my desk, that I have never

                                              noticed before?

                              it's inside a plastic file

                    (I used to call those poly(thene) pockets but had
                    to stop because people thought I meant the toy

I like the name though, pockets, slipping your
hand in at the top, whipping whatever out)

there's a face on it,   the poster,   simplistic

made of a colon   :   rotated   ..

and a bracket   )   rotated   ⌣

against bullying in the workplace   I think

can't imagine a poster with an autoshapes smiley face

                                                made in PowerPoint ?

would do much to stop bullying in the workplace

imagining, my boss, approaching, ready to thrust his hands down my bra

stopping, seeing   ..

                                                        ⌣

AH, he'd say, stepping back, AS YOU WERE,

putting his hands in his pockets as he   if that were the case I'd get

walks away, the poster stopping him   the printer running

from having anything to do with them   print:

him seeing,   ..

                                                ⌣ (me, phew!)

polypocketing them up onto the walls in hundreds

pockets telling him to stick to his pockets

a perfect wallpaper for the office

..   ..
⌣   ⌣   ⌣   ⌣   ⌣   ⌣   ⌣   ⌣   ⌣   ⌣

me at my desk

would be finally at rest

(not dead!)

just   stable

this would of course be a classic time for my boss to
actually appear, hands and all, but it seems (looking up)

that I'm alright   (scanning newsroom)

(just in case)

moving now

(just in case)

down corridor, down

into bathroom

someone washing hands   her,   *hello*

me,   *hi*

(muffled, like I'd said hi with a flannel in my mouth   which would be
weird)

(don't know why flannel was the comparison,

who has flannels anymore? not me,   my grandma did,   but not me)

her hand towel in bin, leaving, me going in, tights down, not really needing
to pee, having peed quite recently, but nonetheless, sitting, trying to pee,
resting on the seat, safe in here from those outside   peeing

lock on the cubicle   a little
as effective as a   . .   a little

                      ‿   done!

and yet as soon as I'm in here   for now   I feel lighter   flush

out, water, waving   hot!   hand red, paper towel, drying, thoroughly,
taking my time, then hand towel, going in bin—   what   seeing
                                        down the side

                      lined paper? poking out

not paper towel   lined paper   weird   do I?

looking back, door shut, hand down   arm down side (ew) (why am I
                                        doing this)

lined paper in hand   looking back, door shut

into cubicle   lock   (paper towel still in other hand

                      forgot to throw it in the bin)

this is going to be disappointing   someone's to-do list

scanning   pulse in chest   thumping!

biro   why am I excited about a piece of paper?

writing angular,

pen fading

and   Gd night Tues foil on middle but lots "treatment"

returning,   Wed nite – incl mild vibrating, woke early,

in and out   could smell her again – always in the morning

of focus [?]   – ear aching, that acrid smell, 2nd [?] running

hard to   bras half the 2nd floor in oxford street devoted

read, skipping down

bored   3 sets of children (babies) in my carriage, eating potato

yet also   declining Lottie's lunch invite: she is yellow and black

neurotic?   but does seem yellow – George late night phone call

sort of   didn't tell him I could smell it again

intriguing, and

well

trying not to compare,

because there's something   familiar   their obsessiveness

someone here, likely on my floor, (so from the newsroom!)

someone here, a woman,   a woman from the newsroom,

a journalist! sharing the same (large) room as me   has written this
                                                    unsettling

admittedly they're all around the corner, hardly sharing their air, but still!
still

someone here is   I don't know   upturned

someone here doesn't feel   quite right

hope it's not her, the R-woman, the kind one,   did it

is that why she's so good to me? she recognises one of her own?   did it

did she plant this here   no!   happen to her

so that I'd know about her?   too?

no   no   I know that is obviously not the case but that doesn't mean
I can't wonder – fleetingly – before dismissing   sound, door, someone in!

christ, right, paper towel down toilet, flush   know I shouldn't flush

wanting sort of to clutch onto paper   towels down toilet but

but also   here I am

I can hardly walk out with the writing,   I can hardly

showing anyone that passes that I've read it,   come out with

what if whoever wrote it passes me!   it, why would I

I've read it now, I guess   come out of the

that's enough   toilet with a paper

enough   towel

          opening sanitary bin   in

          and me unlock

          and out

is she here?   walking down corridor

is she here? is she here?

is it you?   woman walking past, hair slinking

                                ankles! (trousers cropped)

                                looking snappable

                                if she just clipped a door they'd snap!

is it her?   does Ms Ankle Snapper have her nose full of a smell?

picks the phone up to that George on the note?   did it? no

she's gone before I can make eye contact

before I can say in my attention I KNOW!

not her, I guess   could smell her in the morning

sitting   wishing I hadn't put the note in the bin

not me not her   wanting to read that line again

but who   could smell her in the morning

sad   could smell what? warm slept-in skin?

                        or sharp   stuck in nose

                        that lingering vivid even when they're not there

sad for someone else!   (not scratching)

not scratching   (hand under knees)

giving myself just one scratch   three seconds' worth one, two, three,   okay five

four, five,   no, ten

six, seven, eight, nine, ten tearing

when did I start making bargains with myself, adjusting as I go

it's not new, to be fair,   although now, seemingly,

                              an integral institution to my

                              decision in the scratching department

used to do it with the hot tap   (can't reason why, at the age of five, six,
however old I was, I felt hard done by enough to do myself wrong, but
there I was)

on and waiting, hand turning red, hot,

hot, hot, then suddenly cold (still

hot but feeling cold)

there was that guy   (boy!)   at the back of the class

with his compass

running it across his wrist,

reddening, again again again again until

it bled

I was always the witness

really, yes, the hot tap sometimes, but I was always separate, I thought,
cautious

once I'd learnt impulses do not need to be listened to (when do we
learn that?)

thinking, at the dinner table, I want to cut my hair

(excusing self, scissors from kitchen drawer, snipping an imperceptible
edge, hiding the clippings in a plastic box of marbles)

and the next day,

thinking,

no

I do not need to do that

I have envisaged it, but I will not actually do that

is that when we realise how thoughts work?

how fleeting, erratic (not necessarily even part of ourselves) they are? is
that when we learn to say   no   ?

I would like to learn that again   remembering legs

the fierce   no   sharp

no thank you, ideas in my head

scratching? no I'm actually alright thanks

                opening WhatsApp   no new messages

                        apart from group chat   used to ignoring

                        hardly even notice on my screen

nothing from my him   grey ticks

mum's chat underneath   seen my message now   nothing back

mum read, him unread   funny to see them together like that

in my phone   one above the other

like they could speak at any moment   my him leaning down to say hello

                                        mum nodding back up

always forgetting   that they've already met!

mum coming up especially to see him   feels impossible

                                        that it could've happened

our three pints sitting together

my him insisting on the first round, and opening a pack of crisps

like unfolding a bed sheet   tearing the sides to lie flat

          that is   if sheets usually have a heap of salty vinegar inside

mum   listening   taking a crisp   one at a time   as he spoke

chewing   slowly

trying not to crunch, to interrupt   or put him off

watching her   whilst my him stroked his eyelid with the back of his finger

          to take a break from eye contact

me so tuned in to every movement   in case something went wrong

but them   god   so soft   never known people so soft

try to remember that when I'm numb   when I'm here

not always nice though   to know how it was

                                        how it felt

not that they're gone, no, but then   it was only light, different then

then! mum softening a crisp in her mouth before she chewed   our
three pints! all of that   was this year   two months   or
so   ago   me nervous, tense,

when it was nothing   different now   ringing

not counting   intentionally   not fucking counting

                    desk   phone   ringing

                    phone ringing

                    on my desk ringing

interrupting   *hello*

            them,   *hello*

                                is that the newsroom?

sigh,   *yes it is*

I didn't call I'm not   (silence)

providing surplus information   *well good I'm calling about a story,*
                                Nationwide

                                have been restricting cust—

	me,	*I'm sorry but if it's about a story I'm going to*
		need to ask you to email us
	them,	*who are you*
	me,	*an assistant*
	them,	*put me through to a journalist*
fuck off	me,	*I'm afraid I cannot do that*
		I am not permitted
	them,	*you are not permitted*
		to do your job?
		?
	me,	–
	them,	–
	me,	–
	them,	*put me through to a journalist*
	me,	*I'm afraid I am unable to do tha—*
	them,	*I will be calling the editor personally and*
as if		*I will be lodging a complaint about*
can you complain to		*the conduct of his staff! !*
him on behalf of me	me,	*I'm sorry I could not be of more help*
at the same time		

him,   *outrageous! I'm a subscriber! I pay your*

–   *wages! and no assistance when I call the*

–   *listed number!*

———————

handy! because I cannot be the first to put the phone down, just have to sit
tight and wait it out, so thank you, kind man, for sorting my escape route

maybe one day

I'll leave!

(please!)

of course I will   right

move to a job that is not mindless, does not reek, does not leave me stuck
with my boss in my head, memory shaking me awake, just when I think
I've finally cleared him out there again, and on my last day here, yes, on my
last day, a man (honestly! they are always men! I cannot say that, because
I'll be labelled belligerent but yes! they are always men!), anyway yes a
man will call up and say HELLO! I HAVE AN EXCEEDINGLY
INTERESTING STORY FOR YOU! oh do you, I'll say, do you really?
or is it fully based around your own interest and something I'll politely
humour you about before saying oh I'll pass that on to a journalist and
then not, that's what I'll say to him, I'll say, tell you what I'll write the
story on a paper aeroplane and throw it towards the newsroom (it'll land
a metre from my feet i.e. nowhere near by the way), yes that is what I'll
do with your story, except only hypothetically because that metaphor
implies it'll get closer to the journalist than it really will, in reality there
is no chance it'll come into contact with them, no chance they'll stumble

72

upon it and say ooh! what's this paper aeroplane! that's what I'd say except, well, that probably wouldn't have the effect I'd like it to have, it probably wouldn't even register or offend them, and they might've hung up, I'd probably be better just waiting for them to speak and then shouting CUNT! what's that? they'd say, CUNT! (I'd say), would be efficient too, could get through more callers, tell customer services to send them straight through to me, CUNT! phone down on to the next, CUNT!

CUNT! phone down

CUNT!

the thing is though

I don't really mind the entitled readers and wannabe journos who call

each CUNT! wouldn't be for them   really

just for the boss   eh

I seem to have escaped here

seem to be running, jolting, CUNT!ing

I'm restless

not just because of him   (around? nearby?)

I'm hungry too

in an hour   less than! I will eat   upstairs I will find   the regular cheap soup

still haven't told mum! not that   this   having soup at work when
with her old thick soups   me small   the rest loving
them   me squirming

she would say: leek and potato!

or   carrot and swede!

but to me it was always   soup!

just   soup!

at the table   mouthful   sitting in cheeks

forcing it down and hating the thick mulch

little me then would not believe my default now

at lunch with nothing packed   vegetable soup!

potato   babies eating potato on the train   that note! why do the lines

when do babies even eat potato on the train   keep returning

        let alone three sets   sets   making even less sense

sometimes three sets of children   half-remembered

who the fuck wrote it   and uses the term   sets   for children?
how many children even is that?   in the bin and yet in my
                                     head

itching to go back to the cubicle   like her, whoever it is

        stuck in her head, even if she writes it out, still stuck in her head

open sanitary towel lid see what it said again   did she really say three
                                                  sets?

                                                  sets?

want to see but   also   not wanting to rifle

could some of my writing read like   not worth bloody hands
that?

others unable to fill between the lines like she can   because she
doesn't need to explain or indicate to herself?

I know (even whilst thinking) that my writing would make more sense

diary entries that is – notes on experiences or feelings or whatever, not
because my head
is stable or makes particular sense   as if   but

when I write a diary (when I did) or notes (which has not been for a long
time yes great I know) (no not since, nothing since) but when I did, it was
always there – the other – the performance of writing! I write thinking
someone is looking in, translate my thoughts into something a little
prettier, more heightened than my actual head, context handily supplied,

as if the diary isn't even for me, just for those who find it once I'm dead

that's why she's so terrifying   no   unsettling   toilet bin note
                                                                woman

she isn't even supplying an alibi! there's not even the pretence! of stability!

it's all just   nonsense, whirring, not connection and toilet woman
thinks that's fine   ? is too obsessed or observing or whatever to want
to compose something

composed

managing to compose without the c or the o or the m or the p

or the

etc etc, composing without any element of being   composed

not even her punctuation was together

bullet points smudged, extending, turned to dashes, insinuating
connections when they were separate points, that dash (intended to be a
dot?) by ear aching

                                        – ear aching

I would think it was me

writing it and then instantly forgetting

if it wasn't for the fact that I've never had an earache

don't think I've ever really had something wrong with my ears!   so it can't

sometimes water from the shower meaning my him has to say something a
few times, but nothing more than that   following through this thought to
stifle the fact that

I am   hungry   what soup

praying for   tomato and basil

but perhaps too hopeful

perhaps I should envisage sweetcorn

if I envisage sweetcorn

maybe I cannot be disappointed   head travelled back, screen, back to
                                      emails

                                      _____

Tony wanting those stupid flights   **book these flights asap**
booked
                                      _____

onto the phone I go because it seems he cannot use the company travel agent

established

so that he can book his own travel

pressing   extension 3

ring

ring

ring

ring

thank you for calling

I'm afraid we are

currently experiencing

a high volume of calls.

you can expect a

waiting time of up to

fifteen minutes, coming

oh no   *out of my cage and*

no   *I've been doing just fine*

no   *gotta gotta be down*

no   *because I want it all*

WHY is hold music designed   pulling receiver

  to anger people who are already   from ear

angry ! dormant anger yes but brought out by MR FUCKING
                               BRIGHTSIDE

first time I heard this song I was wearing a ring on every finger eyeliner on
bottom lids wet-mouthed wet-palmed (not wet though)

too young to really be wet

it was at the same point of my life

when I was confused at what the fuss

with fingering was about

trying to get myself off, using instructions! I'd heard from the boys! at the
back of my class!

using   STICK EM IN SEE HOW MANY FINGERS YOU
                CAN GET UP

didn't feel exciting   I GOT THREE AND SHE WAS SCREAMING

didn't get wet

was more just like seeing if I could fit my fist in my mouth

except less lubrication

at least you can salivate when you ease it in

what a moment

what an evening   long one

when I discovered (unnamed then) the clitoris

what an evening   felt so right suddenly so right suddenly not so asexual? maybe not fucked up? maybe actually SEXUAL! AS FUCK! fuck!

doing again and again (worrying instead that I did it too much) (new shame for my oversexed self)

fingers wet then

fingers no longer dry and scrabbling

perhaps why I could forgive the boys (and some men later too) (not him)

didn't want to mock them later for their dry scrabble

I didn't know,	Mr Brightside has changed (long since?)
so how were they meant to?	now Mamma Mia— *hello?*
	hello this is Sean, how can I help?
woohoo me,	*hi! account number 3728, cost centre 9226219*
look at me unnecessarily happy because	*can I please book a flight?*
someone answered the phone	*for Tony Richards*
opening email, Tony, him, Tony, where	*of course, what date is that for, madam?*
there! reading it out loud	*27 July, London City to Zurich 10:05 a.m.*
so polite! him,	*no problem, that's available, is it a return?*

                              me,   *yes, 1 August please, last flight*

I feel bad that he   him,   *let me see, there's the 20:50*
hasn't realised

that I'm not important me,   *is there any later?*

                              him,   *I'm afraid not*

                              me,   *okay*

                              me,   *let's go with 20:50*

                              him,   *so all good to confirm?*

                              me,   *that's great*

                              him,   *all good to confirm?*

                              me,   *yes, thank you*

                              him,   *we'll send an email for confirmation*

                                     and can we help you with anything else?

                              me,   *no that's great thanks*

friendly! to the point!   him,   *okay well you've been talking to Sean*

none of the chat some of the operators   *I hope you have a good day*

try and enforce, as if I don't know that it (me,) *you too cheers*

costs 31p a minute to speak to their helpline

they must be trained! to keep you on the phone   not that I care

about the company paying 31p

more them assuming I don't realise   well, done, okay, into emails

confirmation already through

reply, Tony,   **booked those for you.**

cool, move email into   completed

out of my sight

what now what now until the next thing comes in   scratching
what now

s   tights

c   in

r   the

is there a name for the back of the knee?   a   way

and if not does that mean I'm scratching an   t
absence?

c   lines of white

h   rising

not even scratching at all?   through

my own skin cells telling on me

leaving tracks

google   **name for back of knee**

lunch soon!   **12:50**

not exactly catchy   **Popliteal fossa. The popliteal fossa**

but I guess that busts my theory
that scratching nothing frees me
from technically scratching

**(sometimes referred to as the
kneepit) is a shallow depression
located at the back of the knee
joint. The bones of the popliteal
fossa are the femur—**

12:52

a good time, a magisterial time, a time good enough for me, so close to
when I allow myself to leave my desk, yes yes a great time,   realising I
am yet to drink any water today

ah   not ideal   bottle from desk   up

                              fountain so close, can't really excuse   filling

I wonder if my him has texted me   filling

probably not   work work work   but maybe   drinking

ah man yes needed this a while back   yes yes yes   drinking

refill time need some more of this good stuff   filling filling

                                                      drinking

                                                      drinking

                                                      drinking

                                                      drinking

                                                      breath!

                                                      drinking

                                                      drinking

  drinking

                                                                drinking

filling   filling   filling   filling   drinking

        no   stopping   enough

back to desk   checking phone   my him!,   **racing around atm,**

                                         hope you've had a nice morning x

so many gaps to fill   when not with him   always gaps to fill

same for him I guess?   does he wonder what I'm up to? get frustrated at
his inability to imagine me?   **12:57**

                        me,   **breaking for lunch,**

                                 remember to eat! and don't stress!x

close enough to 1 p.m.   **12:58**

        so   lunch!

        past kitchen area

        bearing to the right

        through the corridor

        stomach moving

        jerking

swing doors

    holding it open for the woman behind

        haven't seen her before

        like her trousers

        grey, flecked with blue wool?

her,   *thanks!*

her,   goes through the other door

the other swing door

that I wasn't holding open

she has said   thanks!   me walking

for me opening a door   she did not use

lobby

waiting

for

a

lift

which   haven't seen boss yet today

does   what if

not seem to be   he's in the lift

    coming   ?

?　　　　　?　　　　　?　　　　　?　　　　　?

　　?　　　　　?　　　　　?　　　　　?　　　　　?

?　　　　　?　　　　　?　　　　　?　　　　　?

　　?　　　　　?　　　　　?　　　　is it?　　　?

?　　　　　?　　　　　?　　　　　?　coming ?

　　?　　　　　?　　　　　?　　　　?　　　　　?

　　　　　　　　　　　　　　　　　　　　fuck it

fuck　　it

(as it bings)

(it has arrived)

(but I have decided to fuck it)

(metaphorically)

(and walk the flights of stairs)

(even though it's now here)

up I go

　　　　landscape poster across wall

　　　　　　as I turn to next flight

　　　　　　　　and again　　　　　　　　　　　up!

　　　　　　　and again

　　　　　　　　legs aching a little

now London   five flights of stairs

    now   New York   with an empty
                                                    stomach

now   I don't know grey scape   up   up

and again   up   up

and again   up   up

    up   up

up   jerking stomach

last   one

smelling   fish?

what do we have here

please not

but

there is no doubt, it's on the sign: **Prawn Chowder**

    prawn   chowder

(words already unfamiliar but growing more distant as I say them in my
head for a third time)

86

prawn ?   chowder ?

below   **Cream of Cauliflower**

which   on reflection   doesn't seem so bad

      ladling (eyebrows peaking, just a little, at how the soup matches
the sides of the takeaway container)

 walking to the desk

now paying   *tap your card, darling*

and tapping (darling)   and   walking grabbing spoon

my hand!, container too hot, palm softening, reddening lines,

   switching hands (surprisingly pink!), round to the lifts, sound chiming,
me picking up pace, just fast enough to make it, stepping in

someone else in lift

someone else asking   *what floor*

gesturing to the buttons   me,   *one*

one? christ, should've said first

rubbing my leg against the side

      going down,

                            man in corner

     doors   closed

     and   man in corner

grasping container   hot   man in corner

container   hot   man in corner

intercom,   *THIRD FLOOR*

him rustling   soup fingers loosening

doors   him out

doors   closing

my eyes!   able to move

not stuck, locked, ahead   alone

intercom, now   *FIRST FLOOR*

out,   doors wide,

out

now

out

down

into

the

corridor

(averting my eyes, upwards, away from the red and orange concentric circles across the carpet), upper arm preparing to negotiate the swing doors, nudging myself and the soup   carefully slowly slowly through

I must walk as if I am not checking whether the sofa and table are free,
I have no purpose, nonchalantly wandering, with my soup that is not too
hot and my spoon that is just in my hand for whenever I fancy using it,
purely making a casual parade of the office, bearing to the left, towards the
kitchen area where a certain sofa resides, not that I'm hoping to get that
exact sofa and table I use most days, just after the fridge, hidden behind
the coffee station, and which may or may not be occupied, no no, just
walking, just scheming at how, if someone has their tupperware firmly on
the table, how I can walk (not dejected, not me!) as if I am only passing by,
not turning around,

(approaching now, scanning for a foot sticking out, a coat draped on the side)

I will keep walking,   I decide, walking,   and just go out the other
door as if this was only ever an intended throughway but ah
ahh   free

soup quickly down, hands (now free) seared pink

pot, spoon, just so, in front   laid out, precise, just so, juuust
knocked off-centre

by my colleague walking past   not boss

(not literally knocked off-centre, mind you, the spoon is still there, soup
too, but he has interrupted the process,

eye contact already made   )

him mouth open,   *hello,*

                                   haven't seen much of you, it's been
                                   a while, what have you read
                                   recently?

mind gone,

not a clear head but a blank head, making me question my capacity to
think at all (even though I know that questioning my capacity to think
is thinking in itself but a different sort and not a sort I'm interested in
much), I know I was reading a book on the train this morning, before I
saw that strange man with the teddy-bear dog and yet here I am, searching
desperately for any hint of a book I might've encountered

                    what   *have*   *I*   *read*

I say

pensively

as if the choice is just too

                         eeeeeeeeeexxxxxxxtraaaaaavagaaaaannnnt

and I merely want to select the right book from my shelf that'll interest
him (the shelf inside my head I mean), so that I'm not just delivering any
old thing,

which will only make things worse naturally because my head is still
blank and time for rumination is running out, only implying I am
thinking over what I say, so that now whatever I say should seem more
intelligent – but I still see clearly the table in front of me (my legs
underneath, asking to be scratched), spoon still clean, phone flashing
WhatsApps   greenunbroken chats hiding the carefully chosen
background of my phone (although now I can't remember what it ever
was) and I see him noticing too, looking, without wanting to, at my
phone, flickering,   him to the phone, and then to me, to the phone,
me too, to the phone, to him, him to me, phone, me, me, him, and I now
can't turn the phone over (letting the back face up), because he'll know
that I know and that we both know,

so I let it flicker, whilst I continue to think

still not in my head, seeing clearly what is in front,   and overhead:

him, standing, jutting out, signalling to those walking   lightbulb blinking

that the nook behind the coffee station is in use,

signalling to those passing by, look in!, look at the

reddening girl sitting on the sofa, mouth shut

still me, looking out, locking eyes with the him who is now cocking his
head – unimpressed?

am I applying that to his face, or is he

                  unimpressed?   legs warm

but now I see   oh boy I seeeeeeeeeeeeeee

white

 blue lettering?

an image! not my spoon! not my phone! (although I can see that too, an
emoji of a pig, which distracts me for a second but oh no I am not letting
this go, yes an image, a book

yes)

Yes

blue lettering

That's it, you're doing good, it's what I read last week! that'll do, that'll do,
he doesn't know the order of when I've read things

hm ha har dhahrd Hard Hard – something

Hard-castle? no look let's grab the title you've got that   me,   *well, I guess*
                                        it's funny how you can so easily forget
                                        what you've read recently, but I've
yes yes it's a-coming   *read The Second Body?*

That's something, that's something!
Not what I'd like to pick out for him,   *have you heard of it?*
                                        quite interesting

too millennial it won't please him,

but it's a book, he'll know I'm   *looking at butchers and meat,*

reading, engaging,   *and our existence on this planet*

he's not interested, I can see him   *and how we interact, but bringing*
                                         in literature th—

glossing over and I realise,   as he says   *oh, nice, must check it out!*

that it was only ever a polite question,

I could've said anything (well, not anything,

if I had said Cloud Atlas perhaps he might've

wrinkle the bridge of his nose,

but really I could've gone   he's gone

with anything),

slide phone, WhatsApp

my him, two ticks, still not read

                    me,   **Why is it, whenever
                                           anyone asks what I've read,
                                           I go completely blank?**

no   deleting   he's got enough on   he doesn't need me
                                                  complaining

                                                  last active ten minutes ago

must stop checking   find my way to the toilet cubicle

whilst staring at   it's long past that

                              should be

                                   eleven minutes

I am not going to scratch my skin

I instruct myself,

studying the space between the floor and the cubicle door,

deciding, quite firmly,   chipped grouting by my foot

that I am not going to scratch my skin

                              a fingernail's gap

pulling my tights down, letting my hands, flat, reach down to my ankles
and up, behind my knees,

as I do this I know I am not going to scratch, sliding across the danger
zone (still not going to scratch!) against the back of my knees, not
scratching, stroking, (not scratching!),

can feel

paper-thin

a well-worn phrase but

accurate

here

right here behind my knees

        my skin could be torn so easily

fewer layers

and I feel where it has scabbed

just a little scratch, just a tiny graze   I hear that in my head to a tune,

tickling already   is that a song?

and oh fuck

I have to stop myself, I know I will stop myself so my body scratches faster, gets in more moves in less time, if you're going to make me tear away so soon I'd better get my pound's worth and I   ha   pound of flesh

     Pull

        My hands

           Away

Ah

God that was difficult

No!

Stop! That's you done!

but reaching down to ankles I catch a little scab

and it's free

and on repeat oh

boooooy

and now I'm scratching because I'm annoyed that I'm scratching

furious

feel small

and angry

a small angry itching thing

scratching at scratching and oh fuck me scratching and I must stop scratching AND

Tights up

Stop.

Stopped I have stopped.

Skin

stiiiiiiiiffffffffffff

so stiff

hurts to bend my legs a bit, can feel behind my knees skin relenting, too stiff to wrap around the bone quite right, tearing, paper not made to flex this way

legs moving like a soldier, in front of mirror, face seems calm, can't tell the heat under my tights, me, completely separate from my body,

but still in it

recalling from when I was younger

face silent just like this

when I had   the thing   as I used to think of it

            now   I'm not so sure it was a   thing

let alone a definite article thing

but it certainly happened

a few times

when I was younger

seeing me now, face cold (legs pulsing)

I would look in the mirror (a different sort: toothpaste-marked, pink cup
by tap) and hear rising voices

Wait

that phrase is ruined, it was my own voice, loud, I think, resounding in my
head, just narrating   surprising me in what it, wait, no, me, I, had
to say, didn't know when, what to quite expect

Wasn't the usual way, you know, when your thoughts don't quite make it to
words, gliding over the surfaces of phrases, faster, quieter,   instead
whole sentences appeared

I didn't know where they came from although they fell incessantly

and I remember

looking

in the mirror   like I am now

and being confused at how still it (my face) was, how it wasn't moving
when in my head things were so loud, rising furious right out and yet I did
not move, did not seem to feel or wince or, look at that face! look at that
frozen face (I used to think), prod at it as if it wasn't mine

  the worst part was the stillness   this thought backing off,
now being replaced   looking away from the mirror

(no sound) (no big drama in its departure) as a new thought takes its place,
the previous clotted, trudging off, breaking its own fall, sifting down the
sink, younger self with echoing head submerged as I reach for my phone,
      out of my pocket

flow completely broken, now, thumbprint unlocking, automatically
refreshing my email

HARASSMENT IN THE WORKPLACE

being hit

by   **After routine discussions with HR, we are**

my boss,   **keen to implement an easy and effective**

the boss who lingers on   **way for anyone to be able to report or**

my face for a full   One

                                    can't read this

is emailing the office   about harassment

wants to   two

ensure   three

it doesn't happen here four this isn't real

  still looking how can he

  five how can he write that

  he must realise how can't he

Says he is taking this **very seriously**

  no not reading this

  door shut, walking, back to sofa

  (assured, soup and spoon reserving my spot),

  six

recalling my boss looking at me

Me looking at him

recoiling Looking at me looking now, spoon in hand

And him looking

And me looking cauliflower less bland

At me than anticipated

  seven but lukewarm

And still

Him still, me still, yes, yes, the worst part was the stillness

  eight

him

100

touching

pushing

at first, it seemed he was keeping an appropriate distance

(apart from the first introduction,

hand shaking mine)

                              nine

feeling his fingers   scraping up through my body into my mouth

                         ten

(fine! yes! imagining it then, not feeling,

only a handshake after all

but I knew the pattern,   all women do

and I knew to wait

in case he began

to   edge   )

Aside from the reminder of what I am   (ass   istant,

he said, as he finished shaking my hand, making clear that yes! ha! he can
locate anatomical puns in job titles) but yes aside from the reminder of
what I am and the absence, the absence, knowing that my body can be
reached out to, at any moment, and touched, flicked, painted with great

slathers of yellow and green but yes aside from all this and more and oh
don't get me fucking started on the rest but look the worst part right now
and let me say that okay the worst part right now is the fucking stillness
the stillness the simmering underneath keeping it down, pushing back
down

yes yes the silence the silence the slowing down the opening WhatsApp
to explain consent to men who I thought would get it, at least them, How!
How are they not with me here! they don't even know and they're already
not with me! and keeping strength, keeping expressions fixed, that do
not imply anything, imply always nothing because it's the stillness again,
the carefully selected stillness (whilst in the toilet I tear), face unmoved,
(frantically collecting skin under my nails), teeth tight, chin set against my
tongue

still, as I am now, as I keep my legs stiff, half-bent, under the table,
spooning cauliflower,

still

as if miniature scabs are not forming, as if later I will not extract the tights,
          ever   so   carefully   off my legs,

pretending, as I sit here, now, that later   the scabs, just formed, will
not, however gently I peel,   break   kicking up a
bloody resistance

and that   tomorrow morning   I will not wet the corner of a
towel, dulling the marks across the bed   red to brown

stomach sunk   stop!   clutching spoon

forcing it back down   wayward thoughts

        sinking me

    all of it   stop!

      pushing it down

      not now, not now

grey under my nails, heaping together as I push my left thumbnail

           under another finger

        unmistakably flecked with red

each swallow of soup, meaning   spoon

        lift

        swallow

     enough!

I cannot get through the day, if everything brings up something else

           swallowing

           (enough!)

           down

        getting it down

           swallowing

           scraping last mouthful

                                        resting it in my mouth

leaving it there   pushing it around

left cheek   then   right cheek

                        like wet soil

squelch to the left   squelch to the right

now preparing for the   swallow

getting ready to   swallow

                    not swallowing just yet

struggling,   having to count

down   three, swallow?

                                  two, swallow?

                                  one, swallow?

                                  down

                                  down

                                  (swallowed)

eyes burning a little   at what I'm not thinking about   sitting up

                              walking   bin   in

                    spoon rinsed in sink

dreaded desk   returning   desk

slowing pace   slowing   seeing how long it can take to return

  to

    my

      desk

        slowly

          slowly

            getting closer,

                nonetheless

with my incremental steps collecting, adding up until   I   am

                                     sitting

computer in front   hands poised above keyboard   and

entering password   loading   quick   sifting

                                       emails

                                     deleting

deleting the email   erasing him   eyes flicking round   flicking

                           sipping water   no sign

not thinking about the grooves

                against my thighs

leaving lines at the time

then, thinking about them

then, focusing on them

ignoring everything else

that focus

specific, intent

makes it so easy now to recall

I think   grooves –

                    and see!

feel the desk, sharp against my thighs

                    digging in

digging in but not enough   recalling

          hardly there the next day   suddenly!

                              head knowing to distract

          hardly there at all   having not recalled for   ?

                              years   ?

on my journey to school, every morning,   seeing, on the other side of
the road, an old man

mustard jumper

brown trousers

creased

in lines

walking   me walking other side of the road

him limping, left leg dragging, right leg following

left leg dragging, me following

I'd always slow, falling back   walking in small increments to stay in pace

                him drag, me step, him step, me step, him drag, me step

sometimes he'd be ahead, breaking our agreed routine

me going forward, him going back

newspapers under his arm, him getting closer   (other side of the road)

me, step, step, step, step, to align with him

one morning he was with a woman

him drag, step, her wearing sunglasses, stick

arm in his, them   drag, step, tap tap tap

                          step, step, tap tap tap

            me   step   step   step

there were months of this, seeing him, newspaper or not, dragging and
                                                                    stepping

then, one morning,   no man

I don't know what morning though

because, initially, I didn't notice

he was just gone,

        much else the same

        all else the same

        me same, street same

so I didn't notice

but when I did   I began to wait

and I knew   of course   that he was likely dead

                (his wife tapping alone)

and that was that   I was bothered less by his absence
        more   by my obliviousness

that I couldn't even count   couldn't trace the mornings that he had
                                                                    been gone

less significant than I had assumed

head hazed, sucked in recalling him   significant now

recollection wrapping up though   (not walking, not stepping
                                            now)

something drawing me back out   back into the office

where I am   still

looking up now   desk still here, me still here

and   oh   fuck   boss

fuck   fuck   fuck   fuck   no

but   yes   boss   approaching

thought he was avoiding

                                       him,   *did you get my*
                                               email?

get your eyes off me you cunt stop looking at   me,   *which one?*

my fucking face, stop drinking in a single fuck   him,   *the urgent one*

ing part of me you fucking cunt I will fucking   me,   *which one?*

kill you if you keep with your fucking eye   him,   *the Falkner lunch*

contact,   willing him to stop   *it needs sorting*

he knows he has nothing to say to me   me,   *it's done*

he knows it's done he knows he knows   *I emailed you*
                                            yesterday

not saying anything now, not saying a   him,   *I don't recall*

thing, not filling in the gaps he leaves   –

                                                 –

                                            him   looking

                                            me   covering my mouth

                        trying to rest my hand casually over my mouth

                        protecting my lips from his lowering eyes

                                    arms tight

            recalling

                        tongue   me,   *I've got a call*

CUNT   tongue on my

                                    cunt   picking up phone

CUNT   biting inside of cheek

            dialling at random   looking studious

                                                trying to think

                                    how my face would sit

                                    if I was making a call   raising chin

                                                dialling odd numbers

him,   staring   my phone against ear

me,   shrugging

him,   walking   *THE NUMBER YOU HAVE*

phone tight against my ear   *DIALLED HAS NOT BEEN*

phone tight against my ear   *RECOGNISED*

phone tight against my ear   *THE NUMBER YOU HAVE*

phone tight against my ear   *DIALLED HAS NOT BEEN*

phone tight against my ear   *RECOGNISED*

pushing back down   bile   him gone

pushing back down   bile   him gone

                         warm legs   stinging

STINGING!

burning like fuck! fuck!

all down

back to work, back to work   phone down

me down, head down   no   head up

must keep up   pushing back against chair   posture

                                        immaculate

nice and straight   nice and together

checking phone   mobile now   from desk

ignoring other notifications just looking for   my him

          my him,   **THESE MEETINGS
                         ARE SO LONG UGH**

not what I wanted   not quite the virtual hug   but him!

                                        me, **Pint and a hug**

                                             incoming xx

                    phone back over

ready to return to work   power through

NEW TAB   OPENTABLE

dragging (dreaded) desk drawer open   list of bookings out

aaaaaaaaaaaaaand

CINNAMON CLUB   12:45   2 PEOPLE   BOOK

email through,   BOOKING CONFIRMATION

QUIRINALE   13:15   4 PEOPLE   BOOK

email through,   BOOKING CONFIRMATION

pacing through, clicking, clicking, clicking, clicking, clicking

        BOOKING CONFIRMATION

        BOOKING CONFIRMATION

        BOOKING CONFIRMATION

        BOOKING CONFIRMATION

BOOKING CONFIRMATION BOOKING CONFIRMATION

BOOKING CONFIRMATION BOOKING CONFIRMATION
        BOOKING CONFIRMATION   BOOKING
CONFIRMATION   BOOKING CONFIRMATION
BOOKING CONFIRMATION   BOOKING

CONFIRMATION   BOOKING CONFIRMATION
        BOOKING CONFIRMATION   BOOKING
CONFIRMATION   BOOKING CONFIRMATION
BOOKING CONFIRMATION   ticking off, and another,
        BOOKING CONFIRMATION

all these fucking lunches, all these unfortunate people having lunch
        with   a   cunt

letting him get back, two hours later

                        face sheen   red

            sauna tint

        me always head down

        him louder   practically guffawing

do they get it too?   the hand first   fast   knee, knee, thigh

                        touching, me no, touching, him yes

does he respect their   no

oh, no? does he say? oh sure no problem yes of course sorry

christ   back to this   back to this

                        list done and back to this

knowing all these confirmations will mean him coming back into the office
in the afternoon   ready to tell me about his lunch

him ready to say,   great booking!

did you choose the place because of the waitresses?

him ready to say,   great booking!

that steak jesus christ! bloodier than a tampon

him always licking lips, me always   gritting teeth

knowing he was thinking about me in his taxi back

methodically

coming up with a line that would set my teeth down into my bottom lip

him   smirking   lazy lidded eyes waiting for me to snap

me resisting

him waiting

wanting me to bite

wanting to tell me to loosen up (hands on my shoulders)

him coming in   (hands on my shoulders)

me always imagining   him returning with blood detailing the gaps
between his teeth always imagining him eating like an animal   ripping
through flesh

when the reality is   (under my skin, now

of course   rising

                                               with false urgency

that he's probably well mannered   telling me to scratch cutting pieces of his steak   scratch

bite by bite   scratch)

chewing   swallowing   (hands clenched)

without anything slowing him down   no wayward thoughts making him
switch the steak from one side of the cheek to the next   counting
down until he has to swallow

no   nothing to make him falter   oh enough

what is the point of filling my mind with him when he's not even here,
when he's not wetting his lips   right in front of me

this is when I'm meant to be free   able to think on other things

I think   I decide   shaking head

I am due an afternoon walk

standing up abruptly   chair spring!   purse, phone, card

walking out   shaking head   clearing head   walking fast

          whizzing through and up and keeping head   here

                              keeping it mine, all mine

                      not claimed by anything

                                                beep

through spinning wheel bullshit   into the   A I R

sky cleared up, sun!   sun!   sun! air

right and across road, clutching purse

                                        sun!   steering self

                                           breathing

                            right through body

up   down

in   out

biting cheek

head tight, just above eyebrows, hard   stepping

unwanted!, wouldn't mind lopping off half my head   off

                            might be free then   pavement

                                        across   road

corner shop just ahead   slipping in   tinkling above door

wine up to ceiling   little stickers   poxed

£7.99

£9.99

£11.99

£7.99   crisps!

scanning up for blue   salt and vinegar Hula Hoops

                            toes flexing

                            snatching

                            in hand!

                  can't grip too tight

                  more like grasping

                        walking, counter

            man looking up   *hello!*

                        setting his phone on side

        his phone, facing up,   ringing up the crisps

is playing a video, camera looming in   digit by digit   him, *that'll be 70p*

on a giant pus-filled spot, on a leg?   corner shops always have that

(back? arm?) hard to tell, someone   authentic ringing sound   me

gloved, beginning to apply pressure   everywhere else it's   sifting coins

on the mound (me avoiding sight   just an idea   50p, 10p, two 5ps

of the exploding growth on his phone),   me,   *here you go*

turning round, heading out   him, *thanks madam*

door saying,   farewell!

(in its tinkling)

looking up

the sky!

renewed blue now   wisps of cloud

                        same formation as a toast rack

                        no   a rib cage

eyes back down, pavement almost   crude   !   in comparison

crossing road, opening packet, drawing it open

like one of those paper fortune tellers,   crossing, minding

folded carefully in the playground, inked with the possibility of a future,
selecting different tabs – YELLOW – 64! – until you are told   fingers in

YOU WILL LIVE HAPPILY EVER AFTER   looping hoops

WITH A MAN NAMED BRIAN

                      sucking one finger   crunch

                      and then the next   crunch

                      and again   crunch

                      and another   crunch

                      and another   crunch

man walking towards me   me stopping chewing   suddenly   half-
chewed in mouth   eyes down   shoulders stiff tight

                eyes down   and past   clear

                      licking salt off my knuckles
                      steering round

handfuls now   crunch   crunch   crunch   crunch   crunch

filling   cheeks   salt   steering

ready to return, I guess   crossing

to the dreaded, once more

breathing performatively   sucking in the (dirty) air

       which nevertheless is FRESH!   clean!

reminding myself that it's a feeling

the feeling of – feeling fresh, feeling free, feeling clean,

reminding myself that's a thing,

inserting the words into my head   FRESH! CLEAN!

to see if I can feel them   FREE!

this air right now is just mine and you know what it works, just a little,
I feel a little

      thawed

      I feel

      a little freed

feeling powerful   ?   somehow

with air in me, hoops down me   steering left

            back through, spinning

back past security   guy,   *that was quick!*

           me,   holding aloft   HULA HOOPS

           like a perfect-weighing freshly born and
           wiped down baby

                  gotta get my fix!

him, laughing,   me,   beep

finishing as I adventure past   licking last salt   NEW YORK

LONDON

down

down

lifts round,

through

crumpling   bin   in

ah dreaded desk

not so dreaded right now though   after all   it's my station

looking at phone   **15:18**

only a few hours left, after all, at this desk

dreaded or not

not too bad really   extending tongue, investigating behind teeth

finding the last few pellets   salty sweet

sitting now, then   up   walking, kitchen

with bottle to refill which I am now   refilling

woman behind me,   waiting

me,   refilling

half-full, her silence   stillness filling me   louder her waiting for her turn

120

                                        me giving up mine

water just above red label   ceasing pushing   water stopping

moving   smiling sort of   at woman

back to desk   glugging

                                                    glugging

so thirsty? was only refilling water out of habit but

                    fuck me!   glugging

                    my thirst!   glugging

remembering the tepid water by my bed   this morning?   awake
to a dry mouth then hungover (now, seemingly, fine? fine, as in, not
hungover anyway, I am not fine, in the general sense, I have made that
clear, reserved enough space in my head for acknowledging that I am not
fine) but yes it is the point in the day where this morning no longer feels
like   this morning   and yet it was   obviously   I didn't
have time to dawdle, to float   I just drank water and showered and hurried
and felt okay because I did not have time to feel any other way, a new
tactic perhaps, setting my alarm late, overfilling my time (I know that this
will not work, but I consider it, if only to fill the space where I could be
thinking something else) yes from now on I'll arrive everywhere late, and
start everything late, and oversubscribe until my eyes burst and my head
hurts (it already does, but even more I guess) body stretched until I do not
know who I am or what I want or where I am or how I got here or what
happened to me that time   (hands on me) (mouth full) (saying no no
no no no no no no no) yes that time then   which I am not thinking
about

instead I think   about art galleries   (a decent diversion, no?)

I decide (without much decisiveness) I will no longer go to art galleries
with other people   it is too much   having to
give an allotted time to each painting, staring without seeing, (has this
painting been given enough attention? will my companion suppose I have
appreciated it now?), it's not that I don't like art, naturally, it's just, I can't
like it all, and I don't have the reputation that allows me to be selective, to
walk into a room and examine this one, and this one, cursory glance at the
rest, shake head, and move on,

sometimes I think: art is incredible   a popular opinion

but

sometimes I think: what do I actually get out of it? how much more am I
getting than when I see an attractive person on the tube and take the time
to notice each part of their outfit, clocking through, studying the fringing
on their trousers, and the way they've drawn liner across their lids, before
moving back to staring into nothing, what is the difference, really, truly,
honestly, yes, other times this seems to me a ridiculous argument to make,
one I do not agree with whatsoever, and would not condone – would
frown on if someone were to make – but I cannot stand still,

I find myself flitting, doubting I have   the woman again

the capacity to appreciate or understand,   name beginning with R

wondering if there is even anything   someone is beckoning to

there to understand, and when I flit to   her, away from my desk,

this I fear I will not return, and all   but she smiles, saying the while I must firmly assert that I am   with that smile, hello!

not thinking it, firmly assert my   hello! hope you're hav

appreciation and understanding of   ing a nice day! I smile

art   never allowed to have doubts,   back (a trace on my lips)

and these doubts which I have regardless   but why the looks? the

mean even when I am not having   hellos, does she get off

doubts, I remember that I have had   on it?

them and fear that I might still be faking   (I am being unfair)

it   somehow   think she's some sort of
                                                 altruist

(I am damning for no   for acknowledging the

good reason one of my   anonymous assistant?

only allies in this place)

damning of my ally   interrupted   sheaf of papers on my desk

                wordlessly   a   sheaf of papers on my desk

(seeing the News Editor, walking away   away back to his compatriots,
his equivalents, not a word, or eye contact, or gesture)
                                staring at the pile

collection of receipts stuffed between A4 pages

it is not unusual but   the offence!   the same every time

perhaps now right now   even more offended! because it feels so normal!

without so much as a passing thank you

the offence!   I think

                         have thought before

                         (think often)

                         when bundles of expenses

                         are dropped on my desk

                         for me to process

does he wonder about my salary? does he remember what it's like for
money to be   sore   ? sore topic, sore thoughts, sore because present

always   always   always under the surface (scratching)

                    (STOPPING SCRATCHING RIGHT NOW)

I think not   (that he does not think)   but I must process these anyway

scan them through so that the finance team can ease his bank balance,
ensure it doesn't lose its six figures (or more? less? how much money do
you have if you're rich?)

                              opening drawer

                              taking gluestick

                              taking A4 paper out

unfolding paper around receipts   looking at form he's filled in

**DINNER | POLPO | £218.90 | IMPORTANT DINNER WITH
                    KEY OFFICIAL**

scanning receipts   cod cheek   Bordeaux   probably took his wife

        do cod have cheeks?

I'm joking with myself (I think)

as I'm pretty sure they're not actually cheeks   on   a   cod   right (?)

anyway   shaking head   again   at myself   this time

        at my bitterness

(although at least the bitterness is not directed at myself) (the shaking head is though)

    sticking   shaking head   sticking

    they're interviewing, reporting and the rest

    and here I am   gluesticking

train ticket turned over   glue   paper   stick

repeat with a receipt   glue   paper   stick

playing Tetris (actually quite liking the calm of sticking, working out how to fit the most receipts on one page), turning another on its side, stick, folding edges of another, stick

another stick

another stick   feeling like a child

another stick   wanting to be

new page   stick   wanting to be back at home

s	stick	not now	not as me now
t	stick	then	just an instant reverse
i	stick	back	
c	stick		
k	stick	but not really	sort of
		but not really	

studying the Mentos pack on my desk

not sure why I left

just one   but now   that there is just one knowing I have to save it right until
the end of the day, ever sweeter by the wait, new page stick   imagining
Mento in my mouth   sweet

sheaves done!   thickness of the pages! stiff! (satisfying!)

                       annoyed that they feel that way

hard to resent when it's almost enjoyable   distracting even

walking over to scanner

shifting into top

clicking   **SEND: EXPENSES**

clicking green button with a tick   **GO**

watching pages,   go!

                                           go!

go!

go!

go!

still don't understand how something can be spun through a machine like
that, scanned in a second, whilst   grabbing pile
moving

back to desk

                    chucking in bottom drawer
                    should take upstairs to Finance
                    but don't want to move about
                    more than I have to and
                    besides

                    what do they do with it,

                    all this ARCHIVING when they
                    really mean

                          BIN

done, anyway, all scanned and at my desk, feeling the itch rising

and ignoring   that's done

switching, my phone,   nothing from my him
                                    (he's busy!)

                                    (that's fine!)

eighty messages in the group chat   christ

can't get involved   lost my tongue

lurking

they're talking about   an author?   who has written a novel actually
about herself? but pretending it isn't herself? I wonder how they know it's
her, when the author hasn't told them, do they know better than her who is
in the book and who isn't? that said, I already agree, before having read the
book, and despite liking autofiction! liking blurred memoir! still thinking,
oh stop, stop with the talk about yourself, make something up, anything,
anything, escape from yourself, just give me someone else's sincerity apart
from your own, not your own!, trauma borrowed from yourself reads sore,
feel it in me too much, no distance right now, need   distance
          writer!   reminding me about
          tonight!

poetry event, my him saying   might be wanky

googling her now   (the poet, yes)

nothing coming up   (apart from her Twitter)

                    (her Twitter photo a blurred Moleskine)

instantly making me think of mine

not now   don't have one now

then   when I was first introduced to the term

me at fifteen   something like that

got given it with the emphasis   this is a   Moleskine

emphasis making me feel   important   (cringing already) important to be writing in a   Moleskine

thinking then, yes! yes, on New Year's Day   face pinkening now, already

waking at 6 a.m.! and seeing the first light   squirming already

and deciding, I will record this, on   loading up my personal

this new day of a new year.   email now, knowing I

clicking, searching: **solitary tree**   wrote it up and
sent it

(knowing that line, knowing it's unique)   to myself years later

(not that sort of unique, just unique enough to bring up in a search)

here   click   fuck yes here

cringing intensifying   <u>**The single solitary tree**</u>

I wonder how past me would feel to know I mock her (me), that I'm
embarrassed, wish she (I) were more impressive, more stable, less desperate
to not be herself (there is an irony here that I do not like young me,
because she did not like her either)

It's not like now I laze in joy about what I am,

do I like myself now? I don't even know

but I don't express my dislike so

publicly and I   starting   **I sit on my own, on a beer crate**

(early dew? isn't dew inherently early?)   **Protection from the early dew**

yes and I guess now it's more   **Anything is a blank canvas** complicated, the hating self, I'm

more used to the me I am even

if I analyse   ah yes   I thought it

was profound to change lines here

I used to write and think I was

creating some small, sacred

(quiet) art, write with a brow

I was intentionally furrowing

but at least I was writing,

her (old me) output was

certainly better than mine

recently, far better,

it's easy though to beat the grand total of

        fuck all

It's your hands that sculpt

Nothing ever complete before you've

Reached out and attached a segment

Of your soul

The early bird catches the worm

For now my worm is safely in my hand

Each shiver showing how alive I am

Sunrise lost to a body of white

Its portrait waits, behind,

Residing until another day

little me would believe (quietly) even though she did not like herself that
future me (now me?) would've got things sorted

little me believed she was providing the kindling   (the sort of
for a grander wiser older her to follow on   imagery she'd use)

if she'd been right, I'd be reading at the thing tonight

but I'm not   that Moleskine half gone now, used to tear pages out
whenever I'd discover a notebook a few years later

always looked weird! like a kid tearing a hunk

                         of their hair out

the only notepad intact   a detective case I undertook, aged nine, solving
the Mystery of the Notes

in a little pocket Ryman's red notebook

writing in purple felt-tip

paper notes stuck in, with Scotch Magic Tape

saying   I love her, but I also love Imogen

jokingly putting together scraps from a boy at school who fancied me

more appearing after I began my detective case   always remembering it
as pacing with my notebook, in the playground, felt-tip

observing, these new notes appearing

saying   TOP SECRET INFO   (no info

                         on them beyond that)

others saying DEATH BY POISON IF YOU OPEN THIS   ah

me before paths were taken   enforced

is it melodramatic to consider   what could've become of her?

consider it anyway   where would she be?

not much different really

we all like to fantasise

that we are not SUPREME

because of the unfair effect of another

that familiar cringe for little me, that shame at her feels unfair

         for   I guess   several reasons

  1) yes she's young, give her a break, no one turns out fully formed
  and at least she was trying, aspiring, indulging in some poignancy

but also, more selfishly   although I guess this is all selfish
because it's just me   pondering on myself and not even   one part of
myself, but the MANY STAGES!   OF   MYSELF! thorough in
my selfishness but yes anyway

more (sort of) selfishly

  2) I should probably stop because I know how this goes, the
  shame! and then five years later, I shame on the shamer

I remember the eighteen-year-old self who resented the fourteen-year-old
self, and I resent the eighteen-year-old self now

so lacking in self-awareness whilst being convinced that she was fully
actualised, the final authority on herself

so I ought not to mock too much

to safeguard me from even more embarrassment in the years to come,
when the time comes to mock me – present me – who will then be blurred,
unfortunate past me

to be fair to present me though (take note future me)

I haven't been going through a great time

I think it would be rather unfair, to say the least   switching tab

to mock! the vulnerable!   googling   hmm   how do I phrase this

STATISTICS

yes good start

OF RAPE

IN WORKPLACE

drumming fingers (in the space –   **Half of women sexually**
a glimpse! – of loading)

jesus   **harassed at work, says BBC**

statistics everywhere   **81%**

obviously, I guess,   **75 per cent**

it is what I googled   **1 in 3, says huff post dot com**

not sure this is helpful really   not sure knowing (I knew already) but
confirming ordinariness   is   a   comfort??

don't quite buy the comfort of   all in this together

shit! close tab!   *excuse me!*

man, small, wrinkled chin,   tilts his head

me,   *hi!*

him,   *do you know where EM ZERO ZERO TWO is?*

he says, pointing at a printout (an email) with highlighted **M002**   me, *yes!*

when was   *straight ahead, turn right after that glass office*

the last time   *just over there*

I   he says   *thanks!*

peed?   ?   ?   water bottle resting on

desk half-empty, still not had

enough, need to glug, glugging

glug, glugging

glugging

glugging

glugging

glugging glugging glugging

tepidly glugging the tepid glugging because that is what I'm meant to do
(glugging)

pulling bottle away from my mouth   looking   tilting   last lick
left

lick?   that's not the right word?

feels right but not what you do with the last trace   (lick)

of water in a bottle   (licking/draining)   done!

and now for the pee   treating myself like a baby it seems, ticking
off the bodily functions, tasks completed, one by one, the list always there

(have I peed? drunk? eaten?)   down the corridor

how many times have I done this today

down   concentric

down   fucking

down   circles

down   on this

down   fucking

in   carpet

3 cubicles locked!!   into the last

unable to scratch   (tights down)

because their silent presences   are listening

damn! (or phew?) which one? (both?)

peeing, peeing, peeing, wiping   flush!

all still silent!   synchronised shitters

like swimmers   but less graceful

and biding their time for the audience to   leave

out   in mirror   me!   looking   grey?   eyes down

water on,   waving hand underneath   not bothering to wash

just letting the synchronisers behind believe I'm following the right
hygienic pattern

back out!

down

down

down

down

picking water bottle up (next task!) (next bodily function to be sated!)

back up round to kitchen   walking   pushing tap

                                             refilling

                                             refilling

look at me   being an ordinary person

staying hydrated   who said I'm not doing okay?   me

                         they wouldn't say it now   I would

everyone doing just fine   everyone around here looking just fine

      simultaneity   reminding me everyone eating their meals

that thought I had   the other night

                 imagining   everyone eating their meals

                      at the same time   everywhere

let's think this clearly head-on though

interview myself, eke it out

so, what,

I ask myself,   refilling my water

disconcerted you so much the other night?

well

I say to my interviewer   stopping

which is me   back to desk

I was eating my dinner and I could see through the window in the house across that someone else was also eating their dinner and then, yes yes go on what, it struck me ! thanks for the prompt yes it struck me what struck me was that it was not just me and the couple across the street but so many! loads of people! out there eating their dinner which is normal of course it's an established thing after all but doesn't that freak you out? that we came up with this dinner thing and now everyone is doing it? naturally? instinctively? even though it didn't use to be an instinct?

I mean yes thank you before you say it obviously eating has always been a thing an instinct but not eating dinner? making something about the same time every day as everyone else (my thoughts are the same on lunch and breakfast yes!) (but things feel less heavy earlier in the day) sticking it on a plate and eating it all the same

everyone in their kitchens ready to do the same

oh I don't know

(I see my interviewer with raised eyebrows) (me that is looking at myself sceptically)

it doesn't scare me now it just sounds over the top but then it freaked me out, could feel it rising in my head and it made me wonder what if it kept

rising? you know, that feeling (I know you know, you're me) of nothingness
that feeling of all these routines and things, being on time for trains,
building pavements on top of green, going to work! eating off a plate!
what if that feeling of purposelessness just kept rising, heightening, rising,
getting louder, what then? what happens at the point where your head
should burst? what instead? when the roar hits the ceiling of your head
(your scalp I guess) where does it go next, when it's got nowhere left to go?

is that when you go mad? is that the exact moment when you've lost it?

is that it? head on floor, hands over ears, but still

roaring   roaring

you/I/me

roaring   roaring

I don't know, that's not me, at least that's not me

not roaring yet

things rise yes

but they always subside

subside before they can make any great damage

thank god

hurts my head to imagine

claustrophobia inside your own head!

massive, infinite sky overhead and feeling trapped! shut in! and knowing
you cannot leave it, move away, step outside for a moment

no you're stuck

thank god I rise and fall instead

recur, rise, but always fall

I've been raped! yes, I know

but it's not always there, not at the front

not hitting the underneath, the height of my scalp

just lingers amidst the soil

heavy now I guess if not a little relieved

for not much reason really

relief! it's always that! we're trained to be relieved!

I was raped but at least my head is still firmly on my body!

I was raped but at least I wasn't killed!

at what point is it that I think THINGS CANNOT BE WORSE

at what point do I stop qualifying? saying, yes that happened but at least
THIS didn't

maybe that is what will send me mad

not being allowed to be mad

trained to believe it's never quite justified   god   once more I have
                                                                  to tell myself

                                                                         enough

time passing but alongside always the   enough!   enough!

opening tab on computer   (enough!)   Twitter

someone retweeted
video of a dog
with a backpack
on its back

(obviously it's on its back, it's a backpack,   stop, for a second, to
watch it walk

although to be fair not that obvious,   padding along
given it's a dog)

something good has happened   **Congrats!**

but I don't know who she is and   **THIS IS JUST THE
BEST! HONESTLY**

I don't really care so I keep on   **SO PROUD OF YOU
AND EVERYTHIN**

scrolling   enough!

skipping past   **THE BOOKSELLER
profits down for**

money falling, readers falling, me falling down   the   feed

advert for wine gums

but not advertising wine gums   ?

or maybe they are   I've

already skipped past   painting of an artichoke

TWENTY DEAD

an empty water jug

screenshot of a conversation

where someone wants someone   Trump

to do something so they can   Ai Weiwei

pretend they have a reason to have not Trump

written their essay and it has   content

125k likes but I'm not sure I get it   censored

but I also scrolled past without trying to get it so I'm not doubting

my ability entirely, more I didn't allow myself   to get it   Tove Jansson

which is different   self-portrait

colleague asking,   face hard   *tea?*

me replying,   two turtles on a beach   *yes please!*

her seeing my face hard   that's why she offers me tea

always, she reacts   says something   offers something   as if it's
obvious   if it's so obvious   why doesn't he recoil

step back!

shake his head, break down, shudder   doesn't even gulp, take a trace of
saliva down his throat in some instinctive unease

just the same   heavy eyes   spitting mouth   do I have to re-enact?

                                        haven't worn the skirt since

haven't makes it sound incidental,   do I have to remind him?
unthought on

it's not can't   because I could   can it really have slipped

I could wear it   I will   just not yet   from his head in the first

maybe this is it   walking into work with it on   place?

make him draw back at the memory

it's just a skirt though   isn't it

if my face does nothing nothing will

how much can arrogance do

            can it carry you over the line of consent?

feel the impulse: I want to fuck her   why am I back here

him concluding: thus I will   always back to here

     thinking through without it being my thoughts

              I know none of this is right   none of it

is the impulse   even   to fuck?

 or is it power?   back to him again

if I had consented? fucked him? screamed for him, tongue in his ear? would he have stopped?

him: damn damn, she wanted me, power gone?   god knows   except I do

I do know   know it isn't the case

   the truth is just   too simple to settle on oh stop

no   too harsh to settle on   enough   again enough

   what is going on   in my own head

   am I incapable of making sense

   am I incapable   of being certain

      of articulating!   screen dark

   waving mouse   Twitter there again   closing

preparing for my last task   rest closing down

clock-watching

less a task, or a hobby, to be honest

too committed

more of

    a

  life \\| way

    of

although

despite claiming it's

    a

  life \\| way

    of

all afternoon, I have not been doing it

(watching the clock that is)

(and when I say clock-watching, I don't mean literally, although there is
a clock to my right, on the far wall – far enough not to hear it tick, close
enough to tell

or read

or whatever the appropriate verb for ascertaining the time from a round
numbered thing   is

if I wanted to, that is, I could tell/read/ascertain from it (the clock) (on the
far right wall) but

I don't.

I never use that clock)

in fact

(thinking about it)   (which is what I'm doing here)

I never read the time

using a face

I have a watch   looking at the face as I think about this

                                                            this being that I have a watch

but not reading the time   looking   at   the watch

clearly I see it

                                          white face

                                          black numbers

                                          lines

                                          black strap, left wrist

looking away, back to screen

I have learnt nothing

from my study

of the face upon my wrist

the watch is not a key clock

the key clocks are:

1)   bottom of computer screen

2)   top of my phone

this afternoon, with under fifteen minutes until, officially,
I can leave my desk

now

now it is

that I begin   colleague setting down tea

to clock   too milky   *thanks!*

the clock

clocking

the passing

of the

clock

which is not a clock

unless we mean clock in the broader sense

of a thing that tells the time

rather than a thing set on a wall

often rounded

sometimes tacky

I am watching, this afternoon,

the corner of my computer screen

later now, as I digress, you see,   **17:49**

and it allows time to pass before I can even begin to clock the clock

how many times, I wonder, he/she would wonder, will I cash in on that pun?

how many times will I clock the clock in order to think in my head

oh look at me, clocking the clock

how many times   how long   will I continue to think like this
        analysing as I go   warily precariously measuring what I think

                                        17:50

                                        I use a staple remover

(do these have names?

de-stapler?)   to scrape the skin from

                                        underneath my nails

            doesn't look much like skin

                grey, compacted   could be clay

                                        17:51

He has sent me the   **hug emoji**

I grin at my phone screen

warmth settling

me, typing now   **PSYCHED TO SEE YOU!**

lock phone

upside down

staring **17:53**

intensely **17:53**

at my **17:53**

stubborn **17:53**

clock **17:53**

!   **17:54**

thank you **17:54**

I rub the clay, slowly   indifferently   off my desk

17:55

drinking from my water bottle

Three glugs.

Set it down.

Pick it up again.

Three glugs.

I take the last fruit Mento from my packet,

and chew

milky, raspberry, hard against my teeth but then softer, ground into (a sort of) chewing gum

more pleasant   less acerbic

and swallowing   **17:57**

bag packed

                                                                    17:57

emails shutting down

                                                                    17:59

just seen tea on desk, untouched

one from earlier just behind

swiftly mugs into sink, clinking down

                              a quick few paces away

                                                        18:01

bag swinging on back, helmet from under desk

                                        feels confusing

                                        reaching for helmet

getting myself out of the office   after one night off cycling

swiping my card   as if I haven't cycled in weeks

                                                        or ever

to the security guards,   *good weekend! bye!*

approaching bike shelter   the train this morning

instantly normal

swiping card again   when really it was decided   forced!

by the previous night

  all days have their inheritance   their prior decisions

door releasing

            sometimes not so significant

            just the choice not to cycle, after all

     no dramatic reason why last night

            I had to leave my bike at work

            (simple really,   a few drinks,

            not enough to ruin the head or jelly

(although this morning my head   the legs, enough to think perhaps

was unsure, teetering anyway)   if I am sensible,   I shouldn't cycle)

But now

I will cycle it

it is

now what I am going to do

in a minute

once I've gathered myself

and my legs

      my lovely bike

      right there

politely waiting for my return

clicking helmet on

key into lock,

clank, push, twist, lock into bag

steering   swiping

                  out

yanking dress   up

stretching leg   over

and,

                 go!

cycling

onto the left-hand side

pedalling	pedalling	carquiteclose	edging	pedalling
pedalling	pedalling	pedalling	hand out	turning
left	pedalling	pedalling	woman on	road
pedalling	me	whistling	whistling	to get
her	attention	pedalling	her,	*sorry!*
me,	smiling	smiling	*that's*	*okay!*
pedalling	pedalling	pedalling	pedalling	pedalling
itch under	the strap	under my	chin	pedalling
not scratching	pedalling	pedalling	will he	be there
when I	arrive?	?	?	pedalling
just realised	I've done	pedalling	at least	two turns
without	realising	pedalling	clear	pedalling
my head	is clear	joy!	pedalling	breeze
clean	clear	joy!	pedalling	clammy
hands	well	pedalling	just my	right hand
actually	pedalling	on the	right	handlebar
pedalling	pedalling	!!	pedalling	pedalling
soon	pedalling	soon	pedalling	soon

pedalling pedalling pedalling pedalling pedalling pedalling pedalling

pedalling pedalling pedalling pedalling pedalling pedalling pedalling

pedalling arriving arriving arriving arriving arriving arriving arriving arriving arriving

onto pavement

cycle hoops   woman standing behind the space

                       pouring an aubergine-toned trickle

me   out of her Vimto bottle

ignoring her   onto the floor

ignoring her   seeing

                       his bike!

bag off

helmet unclicked

zzzzzzzzzzzzzzip

(un)zip that is

lock, key, etc, etc, and bike resting   other side of   my his!

clank, twist, lock tight   pull out to check   locked

bag, phone, ziiiiiiiiip

(not un)zip that is

open WhatsApp   my him,   five minutes ago   **here! x**

bookshop just ahead

can see his jacket through the window

       (on him)

the pink of the back of his ears   like the inside of a mouth

me locked on him

walking   walking   into shop and past without observing ready to

    pinch!

pinching the insides of his waist

Him,   me!

Me,   him!

hand on his cheek, lips touching mine saying   hello, how nice to be
                                         touching each
                                         other

                                        hello!

                       soft words spoken

not sure exactly what

I'm feeling his skin

through his t-shirt I can feel it

resting my cheek quickly on his shoulder   *wine?*

                                         wine.

him nipping through the shop (so full, me now alone

watching his back   ha! that new Faber book there,

to have some possession   the one with the woman half-

some sense of purpose   asleep on the cover

training my eyes, to show I am not alone

I have company   I love this shop

that   eyes burning on his back   is my company)

oh god that's the back of the head of that girl who always gets retweeted
                                        onto my feed

man,

clearing his throat, crowd softening, faces turning, my him nudging back,
round the side

bottom glasses red,   raised above, coming back to me

me smiling, him smiling,   *here you go*   *ladies and gentlemen! thanks so*

him hand on my back, me, *thanks babe*   *much for coming tonight. I'm just*

as he positions behind sip of wine biting *going to give a quick introduction*

letting me see   fading out as the guy   *to our poets reading tonight, which*

continues speaking because jesus his   *is very exciting to have here, and*

voice is enough to keep me out, my ears *such a great turnout of trojan*

closed off for little reason, hearing,   *welcoming neurological papers of*

in place of introduction,   *sausage flowers in new system* the drone of words, collected together   *beginning of September*

letters, phrases,   inaccurate

but filling a space as I pretend to listen,   warmth

                                            of his hand

                                            on my back

        struck off course

                as I imagine

                suddenly

                the glass   (safely, firmly in my hand)

                dropping

        red wine marking impact,

        rubber trim of my shoes

                sticky

him   FIERCELY ANGRY

                I am reminding myself

that I have never actually

seen his head

f l y i n g

as he rails against

(me, in this case)

but he's also never seen me drop

a glass   so, what

does my current reality know

oh cling on then   (I cling)

willing it to stay in my hand,

as I see it against my feet

crowd hushed, heads a-shaking

me REEEDDDDD!

still safely holding

a little red though

imagination is   convincing ! !   !

I had this fear Monday night   oh god, hold on

pizza on plates, at my his   keep holding!

kitchen table, me holding   use the other hand

my small glass   too! you reckless fuck!

filled with red mouthful

harmony right here, proper

him grinning

me gri   macing as I wonder if I could squeeze

                              the glass too tight, just when calm

why is it always glasses? obviously I have the

usual (ooh steady now, train is coming, and

you're here, on the platform, inches away

from a speedily approaching train, would take

just

a

little step   just   a   tiny   edge   right   up   to

ah

and train now here   (me still!)

doors opening, thought gone)

but why is it (apart from these and others that we all have)

why is it always   glassware

so fucking minuscule

even if I were to

       drop

a glass

I would have just

       dropped

a glass

in fact

I have before

       dropped

a glass

(many!)

       gla

       ss

       es

       !

and it's never destroyed my life, it's even lent me some time before, when I was waitressing in an old job and not keen to serve a particular table

       (glass remains safely in hand)

shaking head (in my head) (not literally shaking head)

trying to begin to listen to the   not cracking

poetry,

the poet who is a poet and thus

here to read poetry is mod

ulating her tones up and

down, slowly, speaking

words

     with

         this

               pace

as if she is calm, zen

flowing   her,

         ffoooorwards

and back

not bursting into pieces

turns out

I do not have

immense

superhuman

strength

I am the sea, filled up

with you, rushing

back and forth,

you are the sun, pushing me

into motion, pulling me back

and the heat – your heat

you, cannot go out

yes you are the sun

enchaining my heart,

if my heart was broken, I would   *breaking it,*

feel it in my head, just above   *my cunt a chalice; overflowing*

my eyebrows, pressing down, as if my   *I am twine, ivy, ready*

forehead were expanding, growing,   *to entrap you, but just*

stretching across my skull, eyes   *when I'm ready, you withdraw*

out of place, cheeks tensing, pushing   *spreading heat, sticky, over me*

back up to leave space for my mouth   *nipples glazed with your mist*

which it seems I would have lost at some point during the process, quiet,

my him, standing behind me   interrupting where I was going

                                        nudges my back

I turn my head and grin   (I don't know where I was going)

my him, grinning too

us saying

in my grin, his grin,   I love you

                                        isn't this awful
                                        but nevertheless
                                        I am content

tuning back in,   *shattered floor*

                               cock against my tongue

only to be sent fading back out   her fading

great!   her fault   with her bloody cock against my tongue me seeing   cock in my throat

recalling

because of this bloody poet

recalling

him   not my him, not this him, but a him, a person of
the male gender, that sort of he/him, who is not mine, never wanted him,
he was only ever boss, afar, and yet he made himself a him,   forcing
definitions   eyes, mouth, voice all particular right into my

     head and

     has never left since

because of this bloody poet

I'm recalling

him

thrusting   can't use that word

my head over   I think of thrusting when I'm thinking of sex and
heat and JOY

                                 NOT

                             his cock

                   surging up

no

back of my throat now

and now I come to think of it   (still what I'm doing

that's a problem, isn't it   right now, yes, thinking)

my throat, that is

sometimes when I brush my teeth,

hard not to react

to gag forward

my throat resisting

it thinking: yes   I know this pattern

and you can leave

I'll force you out

once and for all

off with you! unwanted penis!   sounds like I'm standing up

trying to take vacation in   to a fucking superhero villain

MY MOUTH   GET OFF!

(bile

at

the

back

of

my

throat   now right here at a fucking poetry reading

it's literally happening now with nothing in my fucking mouth)

christ

fucking mouth

sounds like a pun but it isn't so don't think it   cunt

I'll have my mouth back, fuckless, thank you,
for now, right now, fuckless, as I want it

no   no   no   you never fucked it   no   no   no

fucking is what I do   and want to do and think about doing

                    and am joyed to do

no   no   no   you never fucked it   no   no   no

maybe it's even useful   (it's not)

that I've been raped   (it's not)

because now I can write about it and

when conversation begins, I can take the reins, say

       uh, no

            this

            is how it is

                  (has that ever happened?

                        (no))

so yes, good really, and it's distant enough to not   (it's not)

have affected me any longer   (it does) you just swallowed

                    your own bile

                    have you forgotten already

but I am allowing myself to forget

pushing back down   thinking not of   knees throat   allowing
to digress on my digress because, oh, I know

I do like straight lines really

flowing thoughts that follow linearity

honestly

but dear god isn't it laborious

let me carry on sliding

down

mind changing

flicking

until I'm ready to say   or think   on something

                                                                    c

                                                                    o

                                                                    n

                                                                    c

                                                                    r

                                                                    e

                                                                    t

                                                                    e

I have drifted   significantly

thinking for the sake of thinking

filling my mind   LETTER   by

l e e t t t t e r r r r r   to block out

amongst other things   shit poetry

or

more accurately

                                        my awkwardness

that I do not think she is a good poet

and that I am potentially part of a group

a crowd

who all

unified

are thinking a woman, baring herself (in words! her body is hidden),

is not   remembering   why   why now?

very   on holiday, young, in my first bikini, breasts! just, my

good   body ready to be looked at, it must have been soon after
I left my body for the last time, outside of it from then on, ready to rest
alongside people's eyes, seeing them seeing me, always, always, I remember
seeing – as I saw far off on a deckchair a man seeing me, my eyes his eyes
– a little girl, in the shallow end of the swimming pool, completely naked
(it can't have been allowed but there she was, with nothing on), and I was
entranced at how free she was, how smooth, uncensored her skin – not
hidden, soft, not stretched or grown

I stared and stared and stared, at that skin all her own, her not seeing it
because her eyes were safe, still set in her face, her firmly in her body, not
even a body, did she know she had a body? even though it was hers and no
one else's it still wasn't quite there,
didn't need to be –   me realising now that I was

and then my mum, suddenly   already giving her a body then

close by my ear,   forcing her into her body

STOP STARING AT THAT   in seeing her body –
LITTLE GIRL – and me, looking up at my mum, distorted, made
suddenly into something I didn't think I was   – but – what – no – I –
   not the last time this memory has surfaced no, I know this image, have
seen it many times, watched it play out in my head as I wondered (am I
wrong? is there something wrong with me?), the shame hot at being told
to stop, at mum thinking bad of me, at being warned for my eyes – (am
I wrong? is there something wrong with me?) are my thoughts, my eyes
wrong?

heat, what shame can do, can make you believe, when all I was doing was
mourning my own skin newly dull   newly not my own

     sometimes still wondering   (am I wrong?) (am I bad?)
for those moments where I stared at a girl   smooth shiny   and
couldn't stop looking   hating that mum might've feared
might've shuddered at the thought that I might be different to what she
thought I was

when really   now   she wouldn't remember   it wouldn't disturb her

me now would though me now is when she'd be upset would make her
put her hands over her ears, desperate for   RAPE   not to make its way
in   desperate for   YOUR DAUGHTER HAS BEEN RAPED   not
to fit in

seeing her face screwed up   jesus stop   stop   how did I get
     yes   girl

shame   all that   nakedness

imagining the poet now   already baring herself in words
me now, with my eyes,

  168

slipping off her top   nipples   pink? brown?

moles across her stomach   I'm imagining myself now

                                                 aren't I, and my moles

my him   stroking my back   and his!

                           us in the shop, my him stroking my back

moles   still taken aback by when

my he said to me   we have the same moles!

me, what, wait, what   having never considered before that there
are different types of people who have different types of moles but also the
same type of person who has the same type of moles, but my him seeing
that clearly, so obvious to him

she doesn't look like she'd have our type though,
hers would be more raised, perhaps

patterned in fewer triangles

I'm glad   in a way   that she is no good at poetry   because
I've undressed her (with my eyes of course, nothing else) and in undressing
her, I know that my him could do the same (with his eyes), might have
already done the same (with his eyes), and she looks good undressed (if my
imagination is correct), too good, if she was good   at poetry   as
well as being nice undressed   then I may as well leave now, miss my him
scooping her up (not that he would, scoop her up that is, but still, my head
my head that is enough)

sipping my wine   hitting back of throat blinking   his hand rubbing my back

poem halting   applause starting, me tapping hand against
red-bottomed glass, more a padding than a clapping   if the
others dulled, I wouldn't be applauding, I am being propped up, certified
by everyone else bothering to make a sound

in my ear he says   *this is rubbish*

          me,   mumbling back   *awful*

          my him,   *you hungry?*

is he?   me,   haven't even thought about food   *think so*

          my him,   haven't even thought to think   *I'm starving*
                              about food

                    me,   *let's eat!*

god knows what my body   winding out, gulping last,

wants, although now, suddenly, I can   glass on side, my him ahead

feel the space in my stomach, growing,

building!   my him,   *how would you feel about the chippie?*

fuck yes   me,   *fuck yes!*

it's just ahead, we know the one, his hand leading mine still

          my him,   *it's a shame she was so fucking bad*

deciding   me,   laughing, him laughing, us guilty but laughing later I'll tell him   my him,   opening door

everything   wait   me,   *what do you fancy?*

really? didn't expect my brain   my him,   *steak and kidney pie*

to take me there (following after   me,   *want to share large chips?*

am I telling him?   it, chasing that   my him,   *yeah!*

will I tell him?   thought. really? really? really?

how? practising   can I? dare I? should I?)

(in my head)   oh god   him paying

I WAS RAPED!   me too slow, *ah, ah thanks!*

practising   him, *no problem sweetheart*

HE RAPED ME!   me, *so how was today?*

RAPED! ME!   not saying HE RAPED ME, instead, saying, how
was the pitch and what did your boss say and do you feel optimistic now?
oh good yes that's so good I'm so proud of you babe, me, your unraped
girlfriend, who hasn't had her boss's cock thrust inside of her and her
insides scraped out and her body extracted and replaced with numb, scabby
skin, yes yes no just me your unraped and proud girlfriend who hasn't gone
all weird and empty and desperate for (if I don't say anything) everything
to return back to how it was and yes here are our chips and your pie good
let's tuck in yes yes please do make them a bit saltier, oops yes quite hot ha
ha yes I can feel the heat passing down, a scalding orb, further down and
down down down to stomach, yes water please and thank you ah tepid
how lovely to drink warm water, which is lemony ? ? why have they put
lemon in the fucking water but ah less burny now and fuck me his pie is

good (his but I've dipped my chips in) proper good gravy, rich but I don't know what sort of rich, wine or something in it? but that's a bit fancy for a pie oh I don't know but it's good and look at him look at him stroking my knuckle with his thumb without him even noticing that he is, him beaming and looking so happy and I don't even know what I've said to him I just know it's not I WAS RAPED and I know I'm being good, I'm being old me, and I think that's why he's happy and beaming and I'm relieved that at least I'm relieved to see his teeth and to know he's not worrying in this moment he's not worrying about what he can't understand or work out and that makes me grin too, oh god, it feels so nice to smile and to melt – those eyes, my him's eyes! and these chips! salt perfect, my him leaning in now for a greasy salty kiss that I only want more of oh god how could I tell him, how could I possibly tell him what good would that do, what on earth would that do but crush him dull him, those eyes, dull those eyes to nothing, no I'll get better   quietly, get better, new job first, get out of there first, let it all fade, slowly, fade, fade and then I'll be me! unraped almost   it's not like I was cut open or chained in a dark room for months or years or days or even hours or minutes, much was the same, cock in me, movement, the workings of sex, nothing more, nothing less, yes, sex, practically sex, guilt I can feel at most, as if I am a cheat, but nothing more, no, eating, lying, eating, lying (to myself) (to him?) and eating, does it count as lying? is silence lying? eating, him eating, me eating, we eating (filling) (greasing) (slowing), slowing in my eating, no more chips for me, no thank you (one more chip) (just one more), crispies in the bottom, us crunching, hands shiny, us both sitting back, shiny, slowing, full

ah

full

172

yes

me,   *oh god*

him,   *full?*

me,   *full*

head a little tight, eyes a little weighted, am I tipsy? hard to tell when the
symptoms are the same as anxiety raising its head

feel still, unruffled

seems strange, right now, to imagine   scratching   is that a thing I
do? my legs feel distant not alive   not burning   just limbs, nothing
more than limbs   imagining undressing myself (like the poet earlier
but me now) seeing – not scabs, not rashes, not pockmarks   but white,

smooth, like those statues in marble   hands grasping into thighs,
indents sculpted in, impossibly perfect and toned and gliding skin
later to be able to pull my tights off, dress up, bra un-ping!, pants off (with
grace) (without a hitch) and stand there

say,   WORSHIP ME

him already worshipping, kissing stomach collarbone legs breasts me
glowing him groaning at how glorious   statue-like   I am   him
stroking polished me   time for a pint, I think

greasy-lipped, me,   *shall we go next door? pub?*

          him,   *I was about to suggest that!*

          me,   *just going to pop to the toilet*

          him,   *okay*

up from table

full!

          next to counter

          wooden door, open   so close to everyone else, turning sideways
                              to get in door   tissues on floor

                              sitting

          full   woozy   peeing

                                                      peeing

                                                      peeing

          surprised   peeing

by how much   peeing

I'm peeing   peeing

must be good   trickling

means I'm actually looking after myself   probably   wiping

up   flush   mirror

black marks across

tap, push

hitting soap   nothing

hitting soap   nothing

fine   wetting hands

mirror, not looking   looking

could join the dots with my pores   paper towel against palms   bin

no you couldn't   opening door, squeezing out

I'm being silly   I know   but it's a good line though   table

him,   *okay?*

did I take long? me,   *okay! let's get a drink*

him scooping rubbish, me wiping mouth on inner arm, picking up bag,

hand in hand,

walking out,

across

and in

him,   *I'll get these*

me,   *no! mine! go find a table!*

him,   *oh well thanks*

me,   *XPA?*

him,   *it's on? shit yes!*

me, shooing, then standing: bar

people all around,   breathing

people all around,   breathing

purse on bar, trying to make eye contact   (people all around)

widening eyes, hair falling back, seeing barman setting card machine down, seeing me from the barman's perspective, with my wide eyes, determined (casual) expression

him, *you being served?*

me, *ye-no! two pints of XPA please*

him pouring, me steadying,

waiting, him,   one down

(liquid down its side, delicate puddling)

him,   second down

(head chasing the other)

me card out   him spinning now with machine in hand me   £9

hovering card, done, him, *cheers*, me, *cheers*

back in purse, tucking under arm, pint in each hand, scanning

where's babe?   scanning   people everywhere   shit, where is my
he! where is my he!   where is my he?   what was he wearing?
scanning for familiarity but what the fuck was he wearing? if I was
reporting my him missing to the police I'd have nothing to say, just my
him! my him! in the sort of clothes my him would wear! gone! my him!

   ah there! phew moving with pints now   blue and white striped
                                                       t-shirt!

moving closer, him smiling   that's the one! of course!

sitting down at round table, beer mats, my him, *I was trying to get your
attention!*

hand on his knee,   *I thought you'd done a runner!*

my him, laughing   *are you kidding? and not get an XPA?*

me laughing, him laughing, *cheers!* me, *shame, I could've had both of these,*

drinking ah! drinking! so clean! smooth, glug glug down, bitter tongue, ah!

    me,   *so, today? how do you feel about how it went?*

him, face murkying   *yeah it was fine*

I already said earlier, there's not

did he say in the bookshop?   *much more to say,*

I don't remember   *anyway, more importantly*

why would he ask that!   *when was the last time you*
                                                wrote?

sipping XPA, bitter, bitter   —

resting pint down   me,   *I've been busy, I'm taking a break*

hand on his arm, please not now   *let's not talk about*

you know that look, him softening, a little *any of this*

me softening, him softening, me not needing this, him not needing this,
unable to still him how I used to but still, him softening, head tight my
head tight tight tight tight why always this when I need it least, if I told
him I was raped would he dismiss it? shrug his shoulders say good for you
I know he would not be like that really   really (and yet my head
says he would) (well why don't I try it then hey)

me,   *babe*

him,   concern?   *yes?*

me,   *I'm finding it hard to write at the moment, to keep motivated*

tell him why   *I need you to not see that as pathetic*

you're not going to   wrapping up   you're not going to   sipping

eyes watering just a little, him, eyes, soft,   *of course babe, I know, and I'm*

I want you to be   *here for you, and you'll get back,*

do we? do we all have these moments?   *we all have moments like this*

that we can't tell anyone about? that we have to bury

                                             bury

178

bury

bury

bury

bury   so well buried

that digging up is impossible

spade hitting ground, frozen hard, closed up, cold winter   (it's June)

(but it's also just my head, there's no soil, it's a metaphor, so it doesn't really
matter does it)   him talking, motivating, rubbing back, eyes soft

me drinking beer, sipping, eyelids lowering

I love him, but what I love more, right now, is a duvet over my head

no no stop that

leaning over, kissing, him artfully poking his tongue   tasting hoppy

hand on his cheek   god   his hand on my back

so quick! want him! (breaking away)   woman arguing,
                    (in a pub)   table away
him drinking, me drinking

him, checking his phone   *my dad wants to know*

                                 what I want for my birthday

him, looking up   *what do I want for my birthday?*

me,   shrugging   *me?*

him,   *you're happy with the politics of my dad assuming possession*

                              of you, and then giving you to me?

me,   *let me think on it*

looking at the   *but in the meantime*

rucksack by his feet   *something down there*

stitches across the front   *has passed its prime*

where he fixed the zip   him,   *hmmmm*

or at least   him tapping

attempted to   did I say something wrong?

                        tapping

                        thanks love

            oh!   *that's exactly what I need*

  him phone in back pocket   drinking

        white along the sides   nearly finished

me, half left!   how did that happen

                        glugging

                        glugging

                        glugging

                        breath

                        glugging

                              glugging

                              right down

              him,   eyebrows raised

                              you don't have to finish

                              at the same time as me

                              you know?

              me,   winking

              me,   *is this an appropriate place*

                              to discuss our sex life?

him, air through his nose   *your pint, you know I*

in a silent laugh   *meant your pint*

              me,   *I didn't want you to have*

feel   empty   *an excuse not to include*

not bereft but cleared out   *me in the next round*

              him,   *I can't wait for this weekend with you*

wanting the ease he sees   *it's going to be great*

warm at the thought   *same again?*

but if I say something   nodding

this weekend will

become a marker

a point to look back on   watching him pat front pocket: wallet,

that weekend in June   back pocket: phone,

that was when   kissing me on cheek

watching his back   god   how does he do that

                     blurs it all

looking round   in the corner?

               is that the poet?

had already forgotten about her

(the harshest of judgement)

               her, bringing her glass to her mouth

               laughing, head back

               a lot freer than I expected

               her turning her head

       wait   nose   no

               can't be her

               suddenly

               looks nothing like her

     me   shaking head

           clearing head   arguing,

                                   table away

                                   indecipherable venom

my him!,   *two pints my love*

                     one for me though

      me,   *thank you!*   woman voice raising

                                     with a man, her, heels, bag

me, my him,   swinging on arm, him sitting

pushing eyebrows together (separately)

puncturing her words,   her,   *EVERYONE IN PUB!*

elaborate, dramatic LOUD!   *I! AM! HAVING AN AFFAIR!*

silence cut   *WITH THIS ! MAN !*

            her, starting to door   *are you coming or what?*

pub getting slightly louder, the manscrambling   pausing then   scrambled

them gone, sound loudening   my him, *wow* me, *christ*

my him, slightly raising voice (just for me)   *everyone in pub! I am in*
                                                 love! with this babe!

   so light!   me,   *everyone in pub! I am drinking!*
                                      a cracking beer!

                                                        183

us passing them back and forth back and to each, variants, laughing, eyes
watering light

he's too good   I think   to have an affair

but do they all think that?

I guess so   me remembering to say now   *I finished*
                                                        Atocha Station!

                    my him,   *amazing!*

                    me,   *I loved it! loved the indecision of the*

                            narrator whilst being so authoritative,

                            loved how funny he is, the overlap

                            between humour and and yeah

                    him,   *yeah! like he's actually quite fucked up!*

                    me, *yes!*   him, *and the humour, the inability*

                    to stay serious is why,   me, *yes! the need to flit, to not*

                    connect   him, *exactly,*   me, *god he's great I hate*

          that he's not on social media whilst also being glad him, *why?*

          me, *it means he's writing which is great but it also means he's free*

          of the fucking   him, *mindless bullshit?*   me, *ha yes,*

          makes it feel like he's a dead writer,   him, *yes, exactly, like their*

          archive is done and there's nothing left

184

petering out   not much left to say about the book even though I felt a
lot and so did he but now

I don't know   just not got anything le— my him, *NEWS FLASH!*

news flash!   my him, *this pub isn't a pub at all, but a house, and the*

owners are just too polite to kick us out and gave

us the pints regardless

me,   *do houses often have beer pumps and card machines?*

my him, *ah, but they're beer fanatics and want the authentic*

pub experience from within their own home

oh,

I say,   *well I wouldn't do much, as I've got the beer now, and I'm*

surrounded by people who seem to have made the same mistake

my him,   *no, these are family and friends*

the news flashes build, as usual   me, *well NEWS FLASH this isn't a*

pub or a house but instead a

a thing we established I don't   *hallucinogenic effect from the chips*

know when, but it's built and   *we had earli*— my him, *can chips do*

once simple (once a game of   *that?* me, *they're a very special type of*

BREAKING NEWS! WHEN   *potato,* my him, *we should probably*

EVER YOU HAVE A   *sue the chippie,* me, *yes but for now,*

SHOWER YOU BECOME   *for the moment, you're not in a*

A CENTIMETRE SMALLER)   *house or a pub but a something*

growing, one of those intimacies   *which is an absence and you know now,*

that doesn't really seem to be an   *as I've told you, that it's not real*

intimacy and yet   is   *and you believe me, my him, if that's*

it was how we said I love you   *the case (me, it is, the news told you),*

us walking by canal at night (last month?)   *I'd hold your hand and ask you to*

suddenly (lining up the next one ready)   *take me to safety, me, you can't,*

him saying NEWS FLASH soft,   *because I fear the strange potatoes*

turning towards me by railing   *you ate earlier may not have been*

                    (him laughing now)   *potatoes at all but YOU'VE EATEN*

his hand then on my cheek then,   *MY HANDS GIVE ME BACK—*

stroking   (him saying now)   *NEWS FLASH I'm going to kiss you*

I love you he said, me then, old news   now, kissing   !

me then, I love you too,   me now,   *NEWS FLASH !*

my pint has made me bolder,   *later we're going to fuck*

I still doubt (often, sometimes, rarely)

that he wants to fuck me   that I'm enough

        my him,   *how does the news say we are going to fuck*

now, me, bolder but stumbling   *can we go back and find out?*

pints low, saving stumble with style I think

I wanted to say   my him,   *fuck yes let me just pee*

slowly first, from behind,

then you getting quicker

feeling you hard in me,

grabbing my breasts   (or would I say tits?

me so close to coming   does that sound sexier?

then turning over,   I never know what to

sitting on you, riding   call them, boobs is what

your cock, feeling my   I think naturally but there

clit, and coming   isn't a gravitas to that

coming coming   really, not that there is to

making eye contact   tits, but it feels quick,

with you before I arch   instantly saying sex)

I am wet! thinking about this! and he's back! grinning   *shall we?*

slow kiss, rubbing his knuckles slowly across my cheek   *yes let's*

feeling a wooze, heavy on my eyes, no, not too heavy, more a gentle
pressing, softening, feeling a little blurrier (not my sight, my actual self)
him, his eyes less sharp as they move, us looping, linking, whatever the
word is, arms with me   *shit! my bag!*

unlooping, unlinking, unwhatever,   back to bag   on back (looping, linking, whatever)   getting back to bikes

(I'm not drunk, I'm fine to cycle)

(only a quick cycle anyway, but like I said I'm fine)

walking   walking   transferring   looping   walking

to   holding   hands   holding   walking

him,   *we can lie in tomorrow!*

me,   *ah!*   forgetting   (walking)   that it's Friday ! !

and I'm staying at his! not mine! his! with the clean kitchen and polite
housemates who are rarely in (part of their politeness),

                                    walking

praise fucking be   approaching bikes

him,   *you good to cycle?*

me,   *of course!*

helmet out of bag, clicking on head

key unlock clank twist

locking shut again and into bag

(weight) (on) (my) (back)

him helmeted clanked and twisted ready to go, lovely him with his helmet
pushing his hair up   me,   *let's go!*

                         him,   leading

twisting leg over and pedalling, right onto road   pedalling

pedalling   pedalling   pedalling   pedalling

it's time to tell him   pedalling   him

                                                just   in   front

I could just shout right now   pedalling   pedalling

I was raped I was raped I was raped   pedalling   pedalling

I was raped I was raped I was raped   him turning,   smiling

I have the words but my mouth is closed   smiling back   smiling

quiet and shut and I think it over and over   I can't believe I'm smiling

willing it to rise, force itself out of my mouth   pedalling and smiling

I was raped I was raped I was raped I was   and saying nothing nothing

raped I WAS RAPED RAPED BABE   fucking   nothing

I WAS RAPED   his arm extending left, me

nothing is happening   braking,   pausing

nothing   turning, pedalling

as ever, I cannot say   picking up pace

how many times have I tried?   I don't know   pedalling

I don't know

even when he's said   are you okay?

even when he's said   what's changed?

and I thought   now   now I can say   preparing my mouth

words collected   mouth opening

but I cannot say

(I WAS RAPED) I cannot say

pedalling	trying to stop thought, trying to stop thinking,	pedalling
pedalling	working through how I'm going to fucking tell	pedalling
pedalling	him and what will happen once I've fucking	pedalling
pedalling	told him but never fucking telling him, I've	pedalling
pedalling	thought this through I've done the	pedalling
pedalling	analytics, done the guesswork, so let's wrap	pedalling
pedalling	this up, now, done, done, enough of the when	pedalling
pedalling	how what if but after! after! it's time (not now)	pedalling
pedalling	it's time but no not now, tomorrow, lie in as he	pedalling
pedalling	said and then, with him, arms wrapped around,	pedalling
pedalling	I'll say BABE SOMETHING HORRIBLE	pedalling
pedalling	HAPPENED TO ME AND IT'S REALLY	pedalling
pedalling	HARD FOR ME TO TALK ABOUT IT	pedalling
pedalling	BUT I NEED TO TELL YOU (I'd see his	pedalling
pedalling	eyes, soft, rapt, on me, ready to hear, shocked	pedalling
pedalling	but ready) I won't go into detail, not that I sit	pedalling

pedalling	where it happened every day no but	pedalling
pedalling	I'll say YES, THAT NIGHT (he'll know)	pedalling
pedalling	WHERE I WENT SILENT	pedalling
pedalling	AFTER THE OFFICE DRINKS, THEN,	pedalling
pedalling	YES THEN, he'll know, I know, he knows I	pedalling
pedalling	have something to say, he's seen the scabs, he's	pedalling
pedalling	gently asked, waited, said he's here, he'll	pedalling
pedalling	know he's seen that my boss is dubious	pedalling
pedalling	(a rapist slightly/very different but still)	pedalling
pedalling		pedalling
pedalling	I shouldn't have got myself in that situation	pedalling
pedalling	the thought materialises	pedalling
pedalling	(I stamp it down)	pedalling
pedalling	I am entitled (was) (it doesn't feel like me,	pedalling
pedalling	the me pre-this at the office drinks, who was	pedalling
pedalling	merry and managed to get her boss's	pedalling
pedalling	attention, say I WRITE! I WRITE!, say, I	pedalling
pedalling	AM MORE THAN HANDS	pedalling
pedalling	TO SPIKE, OR FINGERS TO	pedalling
pedalling	COUNT NOTEPADS) I don't	pedalling

pedalling	feel like I'm the woman who believed! had	pedalling
pedalling	the optimism to think she was being taken	pedalling
pedalling	seriously, but no, it is not my fault, wasn't	pedalling
pedalling	her fault either, little, happy, past me, no,	pedalling
pedalling	it was not her fault that she was raped,	pedalling
pedalling	not hers either, I know:	pedalling
pedalling	rape = no consent	pedalling
pedalling	sex with no consent = not sex	pedalling
pedalling	it's rape and it wasn't just rape	pedalling
pedalling	(me quiet, me not screaming NO! but	pedalling
pedalling	it still rape nonetheless) but an abuse	pedalling
pedalling	of power, yes and all that I know, but I	pedalling
pedalling	know (and my he will know tomorrow, my	pedalling
pedalling	he might even acknowledge when I tell	pedalling
pedalling	him) the success rate of these cases of	pedalling
pedalling	vulnerable women against powerful men	pedalling
pedalling	yes no hope we know	pedalling
pedalling	him, money, power	pedalling
pedalling	me, an assistant, silence	pedalling
pedalling	job + no voice / no job + voice	pedalling

192

pedalling   tomorrow I try tomorrow tomorrow, enough   pedalling

pedalling   for now enough   studying his back   pedalling

pedalling   what is he   (turning head   pedalling

pedalling   thinking about (enough) checking me,   pedalling

pedalling   whilst I think?   smiling)   pedalling

pedalling   fucking?   I hope so   I marvel that I   pedalling

pedalling   can switch from   pedalling

pedalling   looking at his back   rape to fuck but   pedalling

slowing   I can and will   slowing

I want that

      (perfect time for wanting) (cycle slowing)

      him right arm indicating   (me copying)

him leg over, gliding with both legs on one side (I can't do that, so I don't)

                   braking (squeaking)

                   letting bike lean left,

                   left foot grounding

him getting key out of pocket,   *home!*

               me,   *yes!*

us unclipping, bikes into house

my him first, then me,

me minding neatly lined shoes

my him reaching for my bike, leaning against his,

(helmets on handlebars)

me pulling his arm, my him bending down to kiss,

pushing mouth against, lengthening as he softens

kiss drawing to a close,

him opening mouth   him,   *upstairs?*

leaving bag by bike   me,   *upstairs*

him leading

                   up   me reaching hand out to bring around him

us up the stairs together   up   up   up   with my hand on
                                                                his stomach

calling out   with that hand   it saying   let's fuck let's fuck let's fuck

into room, light switch on   let's fuck let's fuck let's fuck

me pushing against him, looking up, him arms on my back, mouth
                                                        wanting him

him wanting me, me wanting him more now I can feel that he's wanting
me, pushing against him, feeling him hard, and me   wet

                                              let's fuck let's fuck let's fuck

                                              let's fuck let's fuck let's fuck

him pulling my tights down, scooping hands underneath the edges of my

                                                   underwear

shoes still on, feeling silly that my shoes are still on, but still   let's fuck

taking shoes off as he takes shirt off, pulling tights down

oh god   skin   I had forgotten about my skin

putting his lamp on as he undoes his trousers

main light   off   inspecting skin as I get on bed (okay, scabs but it's
okay, it's okay) looking up   boxers a tent   (slightly comical)
but then on me   nothing funny now   just wanting him, wanting
him and having him! him against me, me pushing back against him
soft back soft back   his ear in my mouth   his tongue   throat
him undoing bra   me arching (to help as he continues to undo my
bra)   him pulling pants   me flexing toes him back over me,
me naked him   that look   making me want him even more
pulling hand down underneath feeling hard oh god   him pulling down
me wriggling further up bed   free   naked and him back   soft
soft   stroking skin   interim pause for condom
preparing   in   in

fucking   !   fucking   !   fucking!   beginning
in my head to think about what I do not want to think about not now

I will not think about it, saying   *let me go on top*

controlling, forward then in and on, moving slowly

                                     sitting up   let him see

fucking   fucking   fucking   (ignoring in head the thing I

fucking   fucking   fucking   read too young in a magazine

fucking   !   !   about cowgirl which now

his hands   pushing up   against   means I think of straw and

my breasts   oh god   fucking   checked shirts whenever I get

fucking   tingling on my tongue   to this point)

can feel the light-headedness surging and a tingling across my tongue
head losing focus   becoming   foggy   oh god

                              his thumb against my clit

this   this   *fuck yes yes*

this   this   this   fuck yes this   feeling close him close him saying

                            I'm close

me saying   *me too*

fucking harder thumb rubbing   oh god   me with my cheek
against his now   his voice in my ear   *fuck fuck fuck*

me numbing, him coming and me   numbing   lost it

reminded of the wrong him and cold all over in my toes and lost it
      his thumb numb rubbing   me arching my back nonetheless
                  pretending   for ease

easier this way   collapsed   us resting

sweat of our legs making my skin   jesus christ scream   taking me away
from him as my legs scream at me   him against the bed, against me

my head on his chest now, subsiding   subsiding

feeling against my leg warm his penis feeling this   warmth! soft now

against my leg   feeling   in that warmth

him open to me fully open and me open too   his eyes are closing
                                              drifting

watching the flickering of his lids   me, *babe*

      flickering   him, *hmmm*

flickering, me gently pushing his shoulder   me, *I'm going to brush my
                                                        teeth*

flickering open open his arm supporting, rising, him swinging off bed me
following   him boxers on, me taking dressing gown from his chair
(always there, always on his chair, I've never seen him wear it, just always
on the chair), pushing open door and right, into bathroom

him following, locking, grabbing brushes, heaping, tap on   water on one

                                      water on two

and brushing   brushing brushing   brushing   (feeling wet, filled up)

                                      sitting

brushing   toilet, peeing

brushing   tearing paper, wiping, flushing

     him by mirror me standing   brushing   him palm flat on

my back   smiling   me brushing   smiling   feeling
okay   is that possible? I am feeling okay (brushing)   the cheap Friday
feeling throughout me   and my him right here with his palm still
on my back   brushing and him brushing and now spitting me first, now
him   handing brush back to him, unlocking and back to room

                                               (sleepy now)

clothes across floor   ignoring   getting into bed   under duvet
                                         warm!

him after me   next to me   stroking my arm   aligning bodies

so warm   so comfortable   this is it isn't it

his head on my shoulder   so close to me

his breathing changing   rebounding as it expels, rough, gargling air

                            him,   *goodnight*
                                    sweetheart

                            me,   *I love you,*
                                    goodnight

                      him,   *you too* (breath) him,
                    breath snuffling, me rearranging
                    and then

somewhere from right shoulder goes a CRACK

I have never heard any of my bones crack like that and it scares me
and he says

                       nothing

198

is he asleep? I'm not sure but I lie

                      here

                      thinking

                      about

                      the

                      crack

growing nauseous   thinking about the crack

my arm has made a sound that has got inside my head

                      crack

crack   crack   crack   crack   crack

jesus what a crack

trying to rest   not think about the crack   him, arms around me

                      his left hand holding my right

      my back against his chest   not thinking about the crack

(exhalation) (he is snuffling) how   how! how does he go to sleep so
quickly! instantaneous, no transition just: asleep!
                  (not thinking about the crack)

leaving me alone (in his arms) to my thoughts   feeling tired   but
here still here

alone with my head   attempting to not think about anything too full-
on, not the crack, nor anything else, (remembering I haven't put my phone

on charge but it's too late now for that), not thinking about anything
no thinking instead about the fact that I am thinking, but of course that
cannot last for too long   recalling grooves in my thighs, the images
have returned haven't they   being pushed hard against the side
of my desk, it cutting into the top of my thighs, focusing on that, on the
grooves, not the hands that were under my dress, not my own voice small
and his tongue fat   no not thinking about that   only the grooves,
that was what I thought of then too, and minutes later, when he had forced
me round, focusing on the empty tupperware sitting at the back of my
desk, looking at the sticker still on its side, on the clips with a logo written
across, a small yellow stain, impossible to get out

my him, his arms wrapped around me, tight

whilst I recall someone else's arms tight,

their tightness meaning   danger   whilst his means   secure

the next day   bruises on my thighs   that not enough

wanting blood   cuts   wounds things that signified damage, that
cast no doubt, my eyes closed shut perhaps, something enough for people
to say

WHAT'S WRONG WHO DID THAT   no question

but instead   weak weary hazed   no longer in my own
                                                    body

I had nothing   I knew then   (know now)

that I had to create, had to form words, a narrative not to explain (there
was no blood, no headline to unpick)

had to find words to unveil – to add, to embellish what my body was not revealing

had to form, have to form, tomorrow I will   form   the beginning

tomorrow I will begin   will open up   (open up as in confess yes but also

open up a mental wound, pick the scab all of that tomorrow) maybe tomorrow too I will stop picking my own actual scabs, maybe that too tomorrow, no more scratching, none of that, no no no tomorrow, tomorrow, words new, nails tucked away, tomorrow, ignoring the cliché of tomorrow (if tomorrow is true, then why not do it now?   wake your snuffling darling and do it now?)   no, he's asleep, me drowsing too, no but I will form

soon I will form, I'm okay now and tomorrow I will form and be okay, further okay

drowsing, eyes closing, ready, honestly, really surely not now but tomorrow, ready

and okay   I'm here   in the secure arms   comfortable   sleepy

on a Friday night   I'm okay   really   really!   I need to speak

    need to tell   but for the moment   I'm okay   really

eyes closing   telling myself that again   I'm okay   I'm okay   I'm okay

I'm okay   I'm okay   I'm   okay   okay   okay   remember that

soon I might need to   lying here still   still

          but okay

subsiding to   darkness

I'm okay

fluttering

head feeling like sinking

falling into the mattress itself as I subside

darkening

subsiding into

okay

now

dark

in dark

eyes dissolving

subsiding

returning

lines of red

Acknowledgements

Thank you: to James Pulford, who supported *little scratch* from its conception, who gave me advice, encouragement and inspiration, and who understands me and this book acutely.

Thank you: to my dream pair of editors, Emmie Francis and Margo Shickmanter, for their connection with *little scratch*, their trust in me and their shrewd eyes; to Cathryn Summerhayes, for championing me and for finding the perfect home for my writing with swift, slick skill, as well as Heather Karpas, Molly Atlas and everyone else involved at Curtis Brown and ICM; to Kate Ward for painstaking, generous and beautiful typesetting, including these very words; to Jordan Ginsberg, Laura Meyer, Sophie Portas, Michael Goldsmith, Hannah Engler, Silvia Crompton, Jonny Pelham, Emily Mahon, Kate Sinclair and the others working backstage, whose names I may not even know.

Thank you: to my friends, once you start listing names an accidental hierarchy forms, but Alex Lawther and Jack Powys Maurice, particularly, for putting up with me for far too long; to all the new friends that writing has brought me into contact with, and who I am still finding.

Thank you: to my family for their warm, unbridled enthusiasm; to the writers who have inspired me with what they dared to do, or did with seeming nonchalance; to the editors who have commissioned me over the years and took chances on me when I had little experience; to kind colleagues. And to my protagonist, who though fictional, now feels real to me – and I hope will feel so for readers, too.

Rebecca Watson writes for publications including the *Financial Times*, *The Times Literary Supplement* and *Granta*. In 2018 she was shortlisted for The White Review Short Story Prize. This is her debut novel.